16

GOBLIN SLAYER

Contents

©Noboru Kannatuki

I've chosen to be happy, all on my own.

"...This much I can be allowed, right?"

©Noboru Kannatuki

GOBLIN SLAYER

❧ VOLUME 16 ❧

KUMO KAGYU

Illustration by
NOBORU KANNATUKI

YEN
ON

NEW YORK

GOBLIN SLAYER

KUMO KAGYU

Translation by Kevin Steinbach ✣ Cover art by Noboru Kannatuki

GOBLIN SLAYER vol. 16
Copyright © 2022 Kumo Kagyu
Illustrations copyright © 2022 Noboru Kannatuki
All rights reserved.
Original Japanese edition published in 2022 by SB Creative Corp.
This English edition is published by arrangement with SB Creative Corp., Tokyo, in care of Tuttle-Mori Agency, Inc., Tokyo.

English translation © 2023 by Yen Press, LLC

Yen On
150 West 30th Street, 19th Floor
New York, NY 10001

Visit us at yenpress.com ✣ facebook.com/yenpress ✣ twitter.com/yenpress
yenpress.tumblr.com ✣ instagram.com/yenpress

First Yen On Edition: November 2023
Edited by Yen On Editorial: Rachel Mimms
Designed by Yen Press Design: Wendy Chan

Yen On is an imprint of Yen Press, LLC.
The Yen On name and logo are trademarks of Yen Press, LLC.

Library of Congress Cataloging-in-Publication Data
Names: Kagyū, Kumo, author. | Kannatuki, Noboru, illustrator.
Title: Goblin slayer / Kumo Kagyu ; illustration by Noboru Kannatuki.
Other titles: Goburin sureiyā. English
Description: New York, NY : Yen On, 2016—
Identifiers: LCCN 2016033529 | ISBN 9780316501590 (v. 1 : pbk.) | ISBN 9780316553223 (v. 2 : pbk.) |
    ISBN 9780316553230 (v. 3 : pbk.) | ISBN 9780316411882 (v. 4 : pbk.) | ISBN 9781975326487 (v. 5 : pbk.) |
    ISBN 9781975327842 (v. 6 : pbk.) | ISBN 9781975330781 (v. 7 : pbk.) | ISBN 9781975331788 (v. 8 : pbk.) |
    ISBN 9781975331801 (v. 9 : pbk.) | ISBN 9781975314033 (v. 10 : pbk.) | ISBN 9781975322526 (v. 11 : pbk.) |
    ISBN 9781975325022 (v. 12 : pbk.) | ISBN 9781975333492 (v. 13 : pbk.) | ISBN 9781975345594 (v. 14 : pbk.) |
    ISBN 9781975350161 (v. 15 : pbk.) | ISBN 9781975376970 (v. 16 : pbk.)
Subjects: LCSH: Goblins—Fiction. | GSAFD: Fantasy fiction.
Classification: LCC PL872.5.A367 G6313 2016 | DDC 895.63/6—dc23
LC record available at https://lccn.loc.gov/2016033529

ISBNs: 978-1-9753-7697-0 (paperback)
        978-1-9753-7698-7 (ebook)

10 9 8 7 6 5 4 3 2 1

LSC-C

Printed in the United States of America

GOBLIN SLAYER

❧ VOLUME 16 ❧

GOBLIN SLAYER

✝

Character PROFILES

"I am to goblins what goblins are to us."

GOBLIN SLAYER

A strange adventurer active on the frontier. He is famous for reaching Silver (3rd) rank hunting only goblins.

"Protect, heal, save."
—The Three Holy Tenets of the Earth Mother

PRIESTESS

Works with Goblin Slayer. A sweet young woman who must put up with her partner's antics.

"Ignorance is bliss, for learning is the highest joy." —Elven proverb

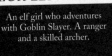

HIGH ELF ARCHER

An elf girl who adventures with Goblin Slayer. A ranger and a skilled archer.

The only things that matter to her are the weather, the animals, the crops…and him.

COW GIRL

A girl who works on the farm where Goblin Slayer lives. The two are old friends.

"How can you go adventuring without pen and paper?"

GUILD GIRL

A girl who works at the Adventurers Guild. Goblin Slayer's preference for goblin slaying always helps her out.

"Before they're polished, jewels and precious metals all look like rocks. No dwarf would judge a thing by its appearance alone."

DWARF SHAMAN

A dwarf spell caster who adventures with Goblin Slayer.

"A naga does not run."

LIZARD PRIEST

A lizardman priest who adventures with Goblin Slayer.

"Train yourself. Kill with the blade. If blood flows, let it be the enemy's." — First of the "Secrets of Steel."

HEAVY WARRIOR

A Silver-ranked adventurer associated with the Guild in the frontier town. Along with Female Knight and his other companions, his party is one of the best on the frontier.

"Only a tangled skein awaits those who carelessly spin tales about love or the universe's mysteries...not to mention a woman's beauty."

WITCH

A Silver-ranked adventurer at the frontier town's Adventurers Guild.

"I won't make friends tomorrow with an enemy I respect. I'll do it today."

SPEARMAN

A Silver-ranked adventurer at the frontier town's Adventurers Guild.

"Love does not consist in gazing at each other, but in looking outward in the same direction." —A poet

SWORD MAIDEN

Archbishop of the Supreme God in the water town. Also a Gold-ranked adventurer who once fought with the Demon Lord.

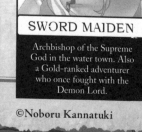

©Noboru Kannatuki

A Knight's Tale

"Lots of knights have taken their first wound at the hands of some nameless nobody! Don't let her looks fool you!" cried someone from the stands, which was followed by general laughter and sounds of approval.

It was a fair comment. There were two riders mounted, in full armor, with spear and shield in hand. One of them was a massive character who could have ridden a proper pony; he was the son of a tobacco farmer and one of the strongest men in the shire. Across from him was a pint-size girl, seated on a donkey and wearing what appeared to be hand-me-down armor.

The bellicose mounted girl had fled her parents' house in defiance of a marriage match she didn't want, but now she was back home. Who wouldn't laugh when she showed up in the lists, the jousting field, as if she was a real knight? One of those puppets with a wooden weapon would have a better chance!

The young man smirked at her, a nasty smile that stayed on his face until he pulled down the visor of his helmet and she couldn't see it anymore. He was no doubt imagining himself easily unhorsing the girl, making her his own, and then heading off to the capital.

How absurdly vain. She swore to herself that she would make him taste defeat.

"I'm gonna send his ass flying!" the rhea girl burst out.

"I keep telling you—you don't have to send anyone flying," said a young man who stood beside her, sighing. He was about her height— tall for a rhea but short for a human. Thin, too. He fiddled with the boomerang at his hip, still not used to it, and muttered, "Are you sure you understand the rules?"

"Sure I do. It's just…" The girl, with her visor still raised and finding the armor rather constricting, turned to her friend. There was no nervousness in her expression; she was relaxed and natural. She was also obviously extremely angry. "I became an adventurer to kick the asses of people like him!"

"You don't have to kick his ass. Just stay on yours."

Wizard Boy looked profoundly uneasy, as well he might. He was one of the "big people," after all. And a wizard, at that. Anyone fitting such a description who came to the rheas' shire would naturally attract attention. The children begged him for fireworks displays while the adults offered him tobacco but gave him a close look as they spoke. Wild speculation about his relationship to the girl with him ran rampant, and it was all but impossible to shoo every last curious eye from around the tent as they got ready.

And to top it all off, the trouble they'd had finding armor that would fit her…

"Rrgh…!" he grumbled, desperately trying to stop the memory of the girl's chest—ample in spite of her heritage and frame— from hovering to the fore of his mind. "Just don't fall off your donkey," he told her again. "If you can both stay mounted, then you'll have to dismount and fight hand to hand, right?"

"Yeah. Which means…" The girl grinned, lowered her visor, and buckled the fastenings as she said, "You think I can win this if we can make it a sword fight!"

"…"

Wizard Boy was silent for a second. At length he spoke, with more than a prickle in his voice:

"Whatever. Just make sure that once you're off and running, you hitch your lance into the rest on your armor. Getting it fixed in place is the really important part."

"Sure, I got it," the girl replied, her ensuing laughter muffled by her helmet. "Okay, I'm gonna go kick some ass!"

Feet pounded. The pounding resounded. People were keeping time.

Feet pounded. The pounding resounded. People were keeping time.

Some people beat against the fence; others pounded their armor, smacked the butts of their spears against the earth. They celebrated the ancient elf queen who had given them the garden that had grown into this lush shire. More than adulation, though, it was pure passion that drove the stomping.

A tournament! A jousting contest! In the entire Four-Cornered World, on the whole board, was there any who would not be excited at such a prospect? It was one of the great entertainments, on par with adventuring, board gaming, and the centaurs' races.

They were just as excited about such a spectacle here in this idyllic slice of fields and tobacco farms as anywhere else. Doubly so because a ticket to the capital was riding on this competition.

In a place where many never left the village their entire lives and even quailed at the thought of going out their door, this was a tremendous privilege. An opportunity given to the shire in light of legends about a rhea knight who had once served the nation's king. A chance bestowed even though the shire had no notion of knights and nobles such as one found in the human kingdoms.

For the youngsters, it was like a dream. Even for this young girl, though she was no son of anything. Those watching must likewise have been imagining what they could be one day or what they could have been once upon a time.

All right, all right. There's no need for all this explanation.

It was interesting! Simple as that. It got the blood running and the pulse racing. It was *fun*! What more reason did one need to be enthralled by a tournament?

When the excitement was at a fever pitch, a judge standing in the center of the field waved the flag that served as the signal.

"Hrrrrraah!"

"Hiiiyaaaaah!"

With great cries of battle, the two riders charged forward on their trusty steeds. (Is a donkey a steed?) The girl put the spurs to her don-key, who brayed and, for a second, reared up. Wizard Boy ground his teeth. But an eyeblink later, the donkey was once again pounding across the dirt, raising a cloud of dust as it drove headlong toward the enemy.

"Go! Faster…!"

A lance for tournament use was, of course, not like a real spear. It was a wood implement for games, designed to shatter spectacularly. That also meant it took all the longer to gain momentum and was that much more taxing to hold in just one arm.

"You…son of a…!" The girl struggled to couch her lance as she bounced in the saddle, fumbling with it with her delicate hands.

"Hah!" At the same time, her opponent easily lifted his javelin with just one of his long arms, calmly securing it in the lance rest.

They would each aim for their opponent's shield, or torso, or head. The shield was the surest hit but not the best choice if your aim was to knock the other person off their mount.

Wizard Boy sucked in a breath and clenched his fists when he saw that the enemy's gaily painted lance tip was pointed at the girl's head. She wouldn't get hurt, not in a million years—right? Tournament armor was heavy and thick. But then that was secondhand stuff they'd scraped together.

She had to be all right. *Go, go, go. Get it secured! Just stay on your mount. That's all you need to do.* His thoughts bubbled and whirled amid the pounding on the fence. He'd never even been this nervous on an adventure. And he was merely watching! Was *that* why?

Argh… Dammit! Just go already! Win it! Do it!

"Hrrrah!"

He heard a clank of the lance settling into the rest. At least, he thought he did. What he heard next, however, was the crash of the weapons striking their targets, the noise of splinters flying everywhere as they exploded. There was a terrible screech of metal, and a shield went flying.

Even in a case of pony versus donkey, that shock would surely have been fatal without protection. A true knight striking with a true spear could hit harder than a battering ram.

There was a shout from the crowd; a woman cried out. Then there was the *thump* and *crash* of an armored body falling to the ground.

Wizard Boy covered his face and held his breath. Damn it all. He would give her a piece of his mind later.

"I *told* her she didn't have to send him flying…"

CHAPTER 1

A VACATION IN THE CAPITAL

"Wow…!"

She hadn't made such a sound of amazement and her eyes hadn't sparkled like this since they'd visited the village of the elves. Which was to say, in her mind, the capital was a place of wonder and fantasy every bit as amazing as the elves' forest hideaway.

There were the towering skyscrapers. The widespread cobblestones. The hordes of people going every which way. All of it seemed to shimmer, her view hemmed in no matter which way she looked. The only natural thing she saw was perhaps the sky, wide and blue overhead. And even it had a misty quality, like paint spread over too much canvas. She'd thought the water town was a big city, but this…

"It's amazing!" Cow Girl said, simply unable to find any other way to describe it.

"Hee-hee! Funny, you stop noticing it once you get used to it." Beside Cow Girl was the receptionist from the Adventurers Guild, her footsteps sounding as light as a feather.

Well, maybe not quite *that* light. They probably couldn't be, considering the fancy dress she was wearing.

Fancy, at least, from Cow Girl's perspective. In Guild Girl's mind, it was probably just an ordinary outfit. She was, after all, a daughter of nobility. Different in every way from some farm girl. Cow Girl was almost embarrassed just to think of them in the same moment.

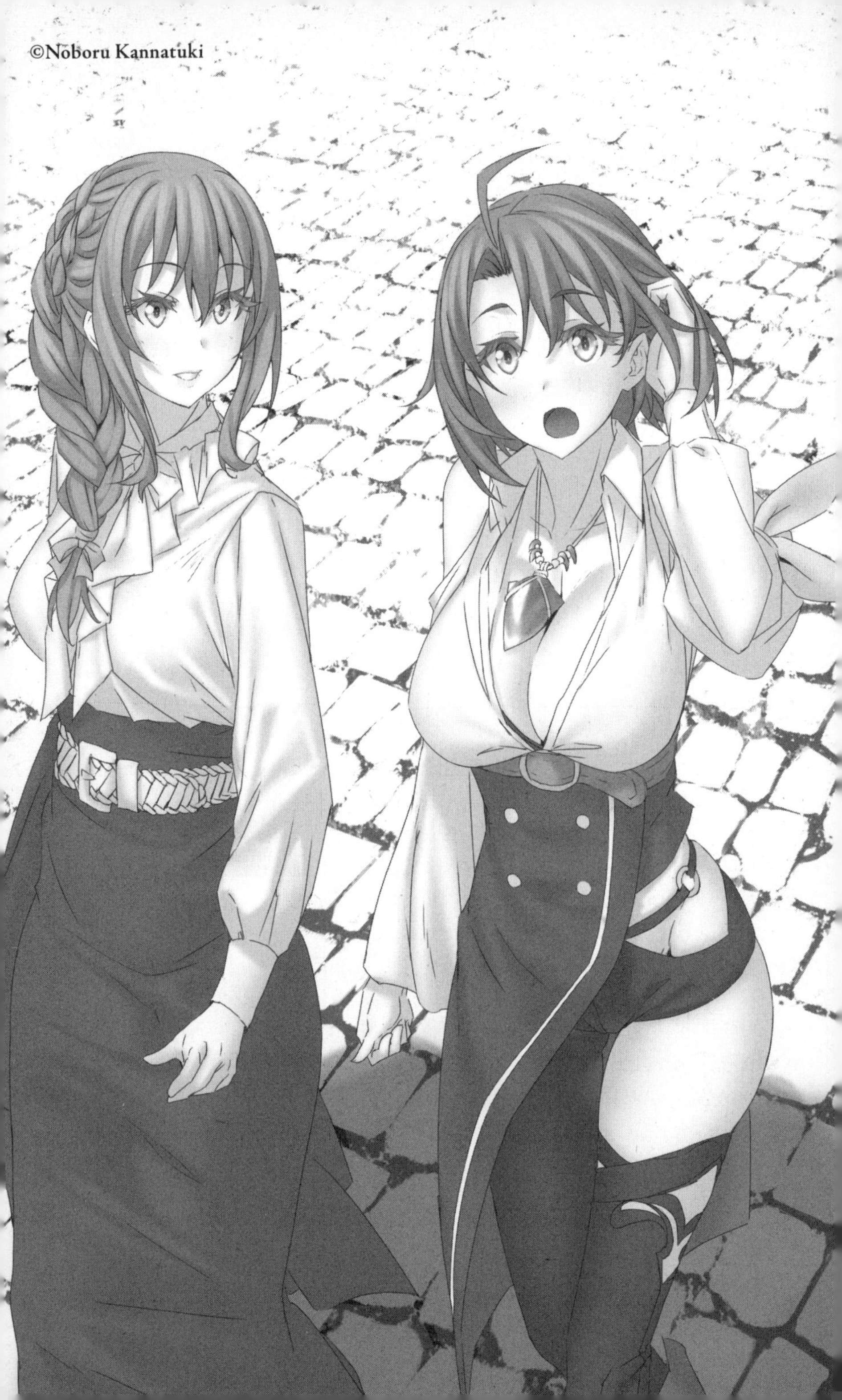

"So is this what elf villages look like to you humans?"

Any sartorial shortcomings on Cow Girl's part could be forgiven, for there was always a bigger fish—or perhaps, always a lovelier woman. Next to a high elf noble, every human woman looked equally ordinary.

This particular high elf noble was dressed in her traveling clothes, which were not so different from her usual adventuring outfit and earned her plenty of stares as she traipsed along the cobblestones. Even the inhabitants of the capital didn't see the likes of her very often, with her shining eyes and almost translucent green hair.

High Elf Archer took the curious looks in stride, her ears twitching. "I mean, strange, and busy, and kind of wonderful. Is that what it's like? One thing I can say—no elf village is as claustrophobic as this!"

"Yeah, claustrophobic from your perspective." A dwarf shaman was walking alongside the elf. He munched on a skewer of grilled meat that he had managed to get somewhere. He passed a stick to the elf, although this one appeared to be grilled carrots.

The vogue for races drew centaurs and their admirers in droves, which in turn spurred the proliferation of stalls that sold food like this.

"Thanks," the elf said, taking the skewer and digging in, stuffing her cheeks with vegetables.

The dwarf ignored her as he licked the grease off his fingers. Then he scowled. "Besides, your kind don't build their own buildings. Just move into hollowed-out trees."

"That's hate speech! Contempt for another culture!"

"Just keep bellyachin'. Wait'll you see a dwarf city someday!"

"You mean, wait until I see a big hole in the ground? At least rhea holes are cozy!"

"And very carefully constructed. Unlike elf tree houses!"

The elf could be heard growling, "Ooh, you!" and the dwarf responded in kind. Soon they were bickering away like they always did. The crowd all around, though, was so numerous and so noisy as to drown out even their customary fighting. Wherever you looked it was people, people, people, people, people, people, people, people, people. They wore outfits of every kind, spoke a myriad of languages, and flowed by on every side like a river. Centaurs, padfoots, elves, dwarves, rheas, humans, and other kinds of people Cow Girl had never seen before.

Even walking in a line along the side of the main road in hopes of avoiding the brunt of the crowd, she felt like she was going to be swept away. It was a flood of colors. High Elf Archer had spoken of "culture," and this was indeed culture shock for Cow Girl. If she'd been an artist trying to paint this scene, she would have thrown down her brush in despair at the futility. It was as if all the scenery in the entire world was crammed into this one vista.

"Look at them all," gasped the young lady beside Cow Girl, sucking in a breath like she was afraid she might suffocate. When they'd first met, she had seemed no more than a child, but she had grown into a fine young woman. She pressed her cap down against her long golden hair, blinking. She was a priestess of the Earth Mother, and now she said, "I'd heard about all the people, but this is unbelievable!"

"It is?" Cow Girl asked.

The cleric nodded back. And she had even been to the capital before! She'd been born on the frontier, but for the last several years, she'd been going on adventures. Even with her burgeoning experience, though, the flood of people in the capital at this moment made her head spin. And she thought she'd been overwhelmed the first time she came here...

"But this is far, far more people than I saw then!"

"Of course. There's a tournament on!" Guild Girl puffed out her noble chest.

Yes, that was it. As wide as the Four-Cornered World was, there were few events that attracted as much attention as a tournament. Adventuring was called the flower of the Four-Cornered World, but people couldn't help but wonder who was strongest in a one-on-one, person-versus-person contest.

Even the gods watched such things with interest from above the board; may they have the Valkyrie's blessing.

"Hoo-hoo! Indeed, I would participate myself if only I had a mount to ride on!" A lizardman priest trotted along, carrying something very large. He'd unloaded it from the cart after they passed through the gate.

"Here," High Elf Archer said, giving him a skewer of grilled cheese the dwarf had purchased.

"My thanks," Lizard Priest replied, taking it and eating the entire thing in one bite. "Mm, nectar! Nectar indeed! In any event, knights and knights only may be part of these proceedings."

"There *is* a way you could be part of it. You wouldn't even have to become an official," High Elf Archer said.

Lizard Priest's tail slapped against the ground, drawing the attention of several passersby. When they realized it was just another excited spectator, however, they turned away again. Everyone was focused on the tournament; they wouldn't waste time looking at the other audience members.

"Yes, representatives have been chosen from every race to compete against one another."

"Ah, I see! For dwarves, rheas, elves, padfoots, and humans are each built differently." Then again, he averred, the heart did dance at the idea of an even fight between different peoples. There was, it seemed, a division for that as well.

Cow Girl let the chatter wash over her as she glanced at the remaining member of their group.

Here we are… Finally on vacation.

At least, she thought so. This wasn't an adventure. Nor was she here on farm business. She'd come to the capital because her friends had invited her.

The idea of traveling was somewhat fraught for her after one very unpleasant winter, but this was nothing like that had been. That wasn't exactly why she asked the question she asked…but it almost was.

"So… What do you think we should do?" Everything she saw seemed bright and fascinating and exciting. There was still time until the tournament started. Although not enough, surely.

The person she asked, an old friend of hers, grunted, "Hrm," and adjusted his grip on the package he was carrying.

He was an adventurer wearing grimy armor; a cheap-looking steel helmet; and a small, round shield on his arm—and he carried a sword of a strange length. People passing on the street gave him odd looks, but he nodded gravely at her and said, "…I'm afraid I don't know."

Goblin Slayer, it transpired, hadn't the slightest idea of how to spend a day off.

§

It started with a scheme—er, suggestion—by Guild Girl and Cow Girl. They had gotten it into their heads to go to the tournament to be held in the capital. High Elf Archer didn't have to be asked twice; her hand shot up, and she exclaimed, "I wanna see that!"

"Yes, it sounds delightful," Lizard Priest added.

Dwarf Shaman, who loved a party, concurred. "Not a bad idea, I suppose."

Priestess, for her part, still felt some reluctance to go to a festival just to have fun. *The last time I went to one of those...*

Well, a lot had happened, and fun had been the last thing she'd had. Plus, this was a jousting tournament. She had to admit, she wouldn't mind seeing what it looked like when knights fought, even once in her life. One of the accomplished female adventurers whom she admired so much was a knight herself...

"I'd l-like to see that...," she said. She had made it her business to try to put herself forward a little more recently.

"Great! Doesn't sound like there will be another chance anytime soon," Guild Girl said with a smile. Having thus filled in the moat, Cow Girl struck the coup de grâce.

"C'mon," she urged, with the proverbial tug at his sleeve. "Let's all go! I'm sure it will be interesting...I think."

"Hrm."

With everyone else agreed, Goblin Slayer could hardly refuse. In fact, the leader of a party didn't possess that much power. He could set the party's general direction, but he couldn't, for example, chase someone out of the group all by himself. As such, Goblin Slayer took a page from the ancient matter of the "nodding elf" and nodded silently.

So it was that they went bouncing along in a wagon from the frontier for many hours until they reached the capital. They greeted the guards, who looked exhausted from all the visitors, and passed through the gate, chatting all the while.

They found lodgings and were just discussing what to do when…

"Let's make up for what we missed last time!" High Elf Archer said. Brooking no argument, she grabbed Priestess by the hand and went racing off.

"Eek!" Priestess exclaimed.

The way her hair fluttered behind her, the elf looked like she was bounding across lily pads. Priestess, clutching her cap to her head, could only manage a "Sorry! See you later!" as she was dragged away. Guild Girl waved to her.

Meanwhile, Cow Girl had a question. "What did she mean, 'last time'?"

"When we previously came to the capital," was all the explanation Goblin Slayer offered. That would have to have been more than a year ago. Well, maybe it didn't seem so long to an elf. "We ended up slaying goblins," Goblin Slayer added.

"Slaying goblins?"

"That's right."

"Ahhh," Cow Girl said. Yes, that would make one eager for a do-over. Especially given what she had learned about goblin hunting during her brief stint on the winter mountain.

She couldn't help wondering about the expressions on the other faces, though. Dwarf Shaman, Lizard Priest, and Guild Girl looked positively enlightened.

"Welp, mayhap we ought to take a little mulligan of our own!" Dwarf Shaman declared and clapped Goblin Slayer on the back with his thick hand. It made a sound like a stone striking a metal plate.

Lizard Priest stamped eagerly at that. "A fine idea. There must be many shops for an event like this. I wouldn't miss it for the world!"

"Hrm" was the first sound out of Goblin Slayer's mouth, followed by "Is that the case?" He was going to let them have their way.

"Very well, then, my two honored acquaintances," Lizard Priest said. "We will borrow milord Goblin Slayer from you."

"Don'cha worry! We'll have him back to you by tonight," added Dwarf Shaman. Goblin Slayer showed no resistance to being bundled off by the two, both of them much more imposing than any human. For that matter, he probably didn't want to resist.

"It would seem," he said with his usual flatness, "that the matter has been decided."

With that, the three men were on their way, disappearing into the festive crowd.

"Oh!" Cow Girl looked like she was going to say something. She herself didn't know quite what, but she felt like she shouldn't let the moment pass. She wouldn't have wanted to stop them, though—to stop *him* from enjoying his day off, his festival.

I wonder how long it's been.

Even at the harvest festival, whenever that had been, he'd been on patrol for goblins.

A beautiful white hand settled on Cow Girl's shoulder as if its owner knew just what she was thinking. Cow Girl looked up and found the person with whom she had shared him during the harvest festival.

"Hee-hee. No worries," said Guild Girl. "There's still plenty of time."

"Um…" Cow Girl thought she could sense a plot afoot. Her heart was racing. "Time for what?"

"Well, since we've come all the way to the capital, I thought we could indulge in some fashion! The latest styles!"

Ah, now *that* was indeed a plot to get the pulse racing.

"Yes, that would be wonderful!"

She wanted to be a princess, but for that, you needed an adventure.

§

The macellum, or indoor marketplace, was unlike anything Cow Girl had imagined. Made of amber-colored stone, it was originally an open-air marketplace set up for *nundinae*, established in a garden to avoid the elements. Somewhere along the line, a roof had been added, and it came to be used for regular markets.

Guild Girl had brought them to one of the biggest markets in the capital. "This plaza was originally built to celebrate an ancient emperor's victory in battle. Today, though, it's better known for shopping."

Cow Girl, who knew nothing about the capital as such, was less interested in Guild Girl's explanations than in the astonishing sights around her. This market, the cradle of the Trade God, was directly beside the library, the bastion of the God of Knowledge. It showed what fine friends the deities were.

The arcade's elaborate construction involved five levels, like a giant's staircase. The roof of each level formed a sort of balcony on which great crowds of people congregated.

There were the smells of meat, fish, food of every kind. Some of the smells Cow Girl didn't even recognize. The aromas pressed in upon them as surely as the crowds. It was a horde of people, people, people, people going everywhere!

People passed in front of her who came from she knew not where, members of she knew not which tribe. They carried purchases whose provenance she couldn't hope to identify. It almost looked like the whole of the Four-Cornered World was crammed into that marketplace.

Feeling like all five of her senses were overwhelmed, Cow Girl began getting dizzy just being there. "This…," she said, her voice trembling. "This whole huge building is all shops?!"

"Well, the fifth floor is an administrative office. But there are roughly forty shops on each floor, so that makes…" Guild Girl put one slim finger to her chin and did some quick mental math. "About a hundred and sixty shops altogether."

"Oh my gosh…"

Oh my gosh, indeed. A hundred and sixty shops? All operating at once? Inside a single building? Cow Girl had never imagined a market-place bigger than the open-air ones that periodically appeared in the towns and villages along the frontier.

"True, it's a bit more expensive than the *nundinae*. But what are you going to do? Come on, let's go!" Guild Girl said.

"Uh, su-sure!" replied Cow Girl, her heart pounding in her chest. She did her best to keep up with Guild Girl.

How expensive was *expensive*? Would her pocket change be enough? Could she afford anything? Should she even think about buying any-thing? Granted, she was too old now for a scolding from her uncle about blowing her money at a festival…

Cow Girl was very impressed by the way the woman in front of her proceeded with sure steps, as if this was all old hat to her. She wasn't sure, though, if she should really be here, given that she was just passing through.

"Oh, it's okay," Guild Girl said, appearing to guess what was on Cow Girl's mind. Her braids bounced as she turned. "You might be surprised how uninterested most people here are in anyone else around them." Then she added, "Anyway, you're just so cute."

"I wish you wouldn't tease me…" That was the best objection Cow Girl could muster, but as soon as she started looking around, she understood what Guild Girl had been talking about. "Y-yikes… A pair of sandals… *Two gold pieces?!*"

"Well, they are very good sandals. Hmm… They *do* say fashion starts from the feet."

Cow Girl didn't have a spare moment to glance at the bustling crowd all around her. She was too busy taking in the shops and their wares.

What's that? And that? And what are they selling over there?

She bubbled with questions like an inquisitive child but forced them back down.

Because otherwise…

Otherwise, instead of being a woman who had come out for a fun time with her friend, she would be more like a kid tagging along with her big sister.

Finally, though, even Cow Girl with all her resolve couldn't restrain an "oh, wow!" She stopped cold in front of a small open shop. Even though most of the locations in this marketplace were proper storefronts, this was a stand-alone, open-air establishment set up in front of a statue of the Trade God tucked between a couple of other stores.

A quick look around revealed that there were several other areas like this, with establishments of their own around them. It seemed that at the gods' feet, one was allowed to set up shop.

On display here were fabrics and textiles more lovely than anything Cow Girl had ever seen. They shimmered and sparkled as if they were treasures in their own right. She couldn't take her eyes off them. Moreover, the seller was a sweet young myrmidon of pure white. You didn't have to be a rustic farm girl to be enchanted by this stall.

"Ah," Guild Girl said, taking a look and pointing. "The wormfolk have come to offer their silk."

"This is silk?!" Cow Girl exclaimed.

Silk: It was the first time she'd ever seen it. She'd had no idea it was such a fine, rich material. She felt her heart pound as she looked at it; the fabric sparkled like a sea of silver sand. She'd heard tell of noble girls wearing silk dresses or even silk underwear, but this...

It's incredible.

She'd always believed silk only came from across the desert on the eastern edge of the world. Had the wormfolk maiden woven it herself?

"Will you...," inquired a voice as delicate and sweet as a bell, "...be buying?" The wormfolk girl turned her big black eyes, lovely and beseeching, on Cow Girl.

How beautiful a dress of this material would be. Fit for a princess.

Cow Girl could almost see herself clothed in the silk—whereupon she waved away a passing thought that it didn't look like her at all. It was so lovely. Such beautiful silk. She swallowed hard. Asking was free, right?

"H-how much is it...?"

"You tell me. Name a good price, and I will be happy to give it to you."

"Umm..."

"Hee-hee! You see, the wormfolk view selling their silk as an offering to the Trade God," said Guild Girl. Just the sort of help Cow Girl needed. Now she understood—not clearly, of course, but enough.

I didn't know there were people like that in the world.

She took the silk gently in her hands. That was all.

"If I may say," the wormfolk maiden began with a tip of her head, "you will be putting a price on my very life."

"I guess I can't buy this too cheaply, then!"

A price on her very life? This wasn't just any minor purchase. Cow Girl didn't even know the value of her own life.

When she informed the other woman of this with an ambiguous smile, the wormfolk maiden only said, "Is that so?" and nodded. She didn't seem disappointed that no price had been named for this, her life. She only gazed at the passing crowd like a fisherman watching the surface of a river. Cow Girl thought of herself on the farm, watching the people going by on the street, waiting for her childhood friend to come home.

Much to her surprise, someone said, "If I might have a look, then." An arm clothed in a fine black sleeve reached past her and picked up the fabric with a practiced motion. The arm belonged to a beautiful woman in masculine clothes, her eyelashes fluttering as she blinked. "What do you think? It would make a fine piece for your traveling outfit."

"Hmm... Yes, it's not bad. Especially since it was handmade by such an adorable young lady!"

The response came from another woman about a head taller than the first. Her ears, which stood straight up and down, flicked, and her eyes sparkled like lightning. She laughed. "How about it, girl? Sell me this cloth?"

"...At what price, may I ask?"

The centaur racer with eyes like lightning ignored the sigh from the female merchant beside her and answered: "One victory dedicated to you."

§

"I'm sorry I've been out of touch for so long."

"You've gotten... How do I put this? So respectable."

The gentle smile on her friend's face as she responded with her thanks showed no sign of exhaustion or edge. It was enough to make Cow Girl very happy; she smiled and clapped her hands.

They were at the thermopolium. This being the capital, Cow Girl had wondered how fancy the place might be, but she was relieved to discover it was nothing beyond her means. A perfectly nice place for four young women to get together sometime after noon and enjoy the cordial atmosphere.

In the other seats were people who seemed to have come from all over the four corners, probably for the tournament. The people were profuse and the chatter was lively; it reminded her of the tavern at the Adventurers Guild that she sometimes visited. The biggest difference was that there was no one here with weapons or armor—only a panoply of different peoples.

I'm sure he *would be dressed just like he always is, even here.*

A mural, drawn with pigments on the plaster of one wall, was very much in the spirit of the capital.

Is that the Earth Mother? Cow Girl wondered.

The picture showed a beautiful, amply endowed goddess with wings. But for reasons Cow Girl didn't understand, the wings were partially covered with cloth.

Strange.

"I certainly never expected to run into you here," Guild Girl was saying.

"Me neither. Although I did get some letters from those kids that mentioned you would be coming to see the tournament."

"I guess we owe it to the dice of Fate and Chance."

"Indeed we do."

Even as Cow Girl was busy being entranced by the environs, Guild Girl and Female Merchant were having a lively conversation. They both came from nobility; no doubt they were used to places like this.

A waitress dressed in finery of her own came to take their order, but even then they acted as if all was ordinary. Cow Girl was deeply impressed. She, for her part, stumbled over her order—frankly, she hardly understood what was on the menu. For example, she was sure she'd just heard Guild Girl order "glires." What in the world was that?

Cow Girl was full of questions—and curiosity. Guild Girl saw her and nodded. "Ah! It's a stuffed, roasted dormouse," she explained.

"Dormouse?!" Cow Girl had no idea you could eat those.

Guild Girl giggled at her surprise while Female Merchant said, "In that case…," and pointed at the menu. "The steamed flamingo's tongue is particularly exquisite."

"Flamingo…?" What was that? Cow Girl was nothing but confused. She was aware it was some kind of bird, but if you could eat its tongue, then it must be very big. Was it the size of a cow's tongue?

Hmm. The centaur racer snorted, then indicated the part of the menu dealing with vegetables. "I'll take the silphium salad, I believe. Gives you energy."

"Take care not to eat too much of that," Female Merchant said, heading off the excited diner before she could race down the menu. "At one point, there was a racer who used silphium regularly to treat asthma and was booted out for it at inspection."

"Yes, because it does indeed make one stronger. It's also said to have aphrodisiac effects in humans..." The racer asked if Female Merchant wouldn't like to try a mouthful, to which the merchant simply replied, "Stop that," her expression difficult to read.

What about leg of giraffe? They were out today. Really? That's a shame. So went the conversation between Guild Girl and Female Merchant.

Cow Girl listened to them with one ear as she industriously studied the menu. She blinked at camel's hump—you could eat those lumpy donkeys?!—but then she spotted something else.

"This is fish, right, not pork? It says something about sausage?"

"Ah," said the waitress, a padfoot. (Even here in the capital!) "That's delphinus. Delphinus salsus. It's quite good!" The waitress's ears twitched as she explained.

"I'll try that, then." Cow Girl didn't have a lot of chances to eat fish, after all. Might as well take this one. She had no idea what kind of fish it was, but as long as she was having a meal in the capital, she might as well try something unusual.

"And to drink?" the waitress asked.

"I know it's only noon," Guild Girl said with an embarrassed chuckle. "But I think I might have a bit of wine."

"For me," Female Merchant said, "aqua mulsa."

"My, you're sure?"

"Yes, yes. Bumpkins' wine, I know. When you deal in as much of it as I do, though, you realize it's quite a lovely drink."

"Sheer hubris, describing everywhere grapes don't grow as bumpkin territory," the centaur said with a laugh. "I'll have one of the same, then."

Cow Girl thought she recalled that aqua mulsa, or honey water, was produced by the people of the north. She knew that the jar of wine *he'd* brought as a gift from those parts was no longer quite full...

Her uncle abstained, for reasons she didn't know, so *he* and she enjoyed it by themselves.

It doesn't really seem like alcohol, though...

"Wonder if there's anything sweet around here," the centaur mused.

"I can offer you sapa or defrutum," the waitress said. "Grape syrup or syrup of other fruits. What would you like?"

"Hmm... Fruit defrutum, then."

"Excellent choice." The waitress executed an elegant bow and withdrew. Cow Girl finally let herself exhale.

Still...

"Something on your mind?"

"Oh, n-nothing!" Cow Girl said, waving away the question as those lightning eyes focused on her. "It's just, earlier you talked about a victory. So I was wondering if you're going to be in the tournament, too." This centaur was, after all, one of the very best in the water town. Wasn't that the reason for the glances she seemed to attract?

Nonetheless, Cow Girl found her affable and easy to get along with. Maybe that was because the centaur's bottom half so closely resembled the animals Cow Girl was used to working with.

"No, I'm an auriga. Not a sonipes."

"Um...?"

"My legs are trained for running fast. I don't know how to wield a spear." That was why the most she could offer the wormfolk girl was victory in a race.

"She's a thoroughbred, a bloodline devoted exclusively to running very fast," Guild Girl added. She said that centaurs who raced devoted their lineages to being quick.

That, Cow Girl understood. After all, it was obvious from a glance at the runner's legs. They were so thin, so angular, so lean and beautiful—but also singularly unsuited to carrying heavy objects. They looked delicate, almost like glass. Beautiful but fragile.

"I sure wish I could see you run," Cow Girl said.

"Hoh-hoh. Now, that is an honor. I promise I'll invite you to the Circus Maximus someday when I'm running."

Cow Girl thought back to the iron horseshoe he'd come back with not long ago. It had belonged to a runner named Silver Blaze. Even Cow Girl, however, realized it would be uncouth to ask which of them was faster. Still, she couldn't help wondering what the lightning-eyed

©Noboru Kannatuki

centaur's legs looked like and found herself stealing glances under the table.

The racer's legs were positioned in front of and behind her belly—perhaps that was the right way to put it—and were folded on the floor.

They should have chairs for the different kinds of people who come here.

"Aren't you uncomfortable, sitting like that?" Cow Girl asked.

"Hmm? Ah…," the lightning-eyed woman replied, shifting ever so slightly. "Just a little, I suppose."

"I'm sure they used to have seats for centaurs…," Guild Girl said hesitantly, her eyes darting around the restaurant. They could see birdfolk who found the backs of the chairs a challenge for their wings and other padfoots who struggled with where to put their tails.

"Supposedly, having padfoots use special chairs would constitute discrimination," Female Merchant broke in. "Of course, everyone has their differences. It seems there's much hand-wringing these days."

"I'm sure sooner or later, people are going to claim it's inhumane to make centaurs race," said the racer. "Even though we enjoy it." She snorted. Horses could be moody creatures. Were centaurs the same? Obviously still angry, the racer rested her chin in her hands (not very good manners) and complained, "'Don't do this! Do that! Be considerate of this!' It's gotten suffocating in the capital lately."

"Things are a bit smoother in the water town. They have the archbishop overseeing things," Guild Girl said, trying to bring some levity back to the conversation by bringing up her colleague.

"She understands that human laws are imperfect," added Female Merchant. "Or at least, that's my colleague's interpretation."

They talked of adventures; they talked of the world; they talked of veritably everything. Cow Girl often found she didn't follow.

But maybe this would be a good idea?

Chairs for centaurs. Not so much chairs but cushions? They could make them at home, sell them themselves. All right, it wouldn't be easy, but… Hmm.

She was thinking it over when her gaze met the racer's.

"Incidentally," the centaur said, her eyes shining, "aren't you going to buy a dress or something?"

"Er… Maybe not…" Cow Girl scratched her cheek so as not to

show she was a bit embarrassed and shook her head. "I'm not really… I mean, I don't know much about fashion."

"Let me come and direct you!"

"…Are you sure?"

"Sure as sure can be!" The racer nodded firmly. Then she took the hesitant young lady's hand and gave her a winning smile. "Nothing in the Four-Cornered World is more important than having fun together!"

§

"Kinda…suffocating, huh?"

"Definitely…"

High Elf Archer and Priestess made their way through the throngs, glancing at each other and nodding their agreement.

It wasn't that there had been any specific trouble. Priestess didn't even have her chain mail to worry about like she had last time. Indeed, the two young ladies were enjoying themselves immensely, taking in the sight of the capital in the grip of tournament fever.

Technically, their most important objective was to find flowers or candy to use as an offering, but be that as it may, for all intents and purposes, they were right in the middle of a festival. You didn't have to be a wonder-struck high elf to enjoy that—just a young woman with an open heart.

There was food of every kind, from grilled apples to the cooked meat of creatures from foreign lands. This being a tournament, there were books featuring compilations of the stories of famous and capable knights.

"I think we'd better buy one," High Elf Archer said. "Since we're going to see them fight and all!"

"Yes… Since we've come all this way!"

Since we've come all this way: a phrase as potent as any wizard's words of true power. They purchased one of the crudely printed volumes and started flipping through it, making sounds of amazement at the crests and the histories of the knights.

There were a great many traveling knights these days; the capital had attracted quite a few who had gone from place to place, plying their trade. They weren't the knights-errant of the days of old, but those lordless warriors were one of the templates for today's adventurers.

Still…

Knights… Wow…

It seemed that the female knight whom Priestess so respected wasn't going to be part of this tournament. Maybe because finding armor, getting a horse, and caring for the same was a great deal of trouble. Supporting all that on an adventurer's income, even one who earned well, would not be easy.

Priestess pictured herself on horseback as she rode to her next goblin hunt and giggled. *It was fun adventuring with that centaur, but I don't know…*

They went along, gawking and chatting, and nothing remarkable happened. Eventually, among the other attractions, High Elf Archer spotted one particular stall.

"Oh my gosh! Look at that! Do you see that?"

Her eyes had alighted on a hat made of wool. She beckoned Priestess over, and the young cleric trotted up and looked at the item. "Wow! Is this…a helmet?"

Indeed: Packed into the shop were hats of every description, from every place and era. There were bowl-shaped helmets, exotic pieces with huge crests, and even some with protruding visors. There were horned helmets from the north—that put a smile on Priestess's face. Yes, that was what their headwear looked like up there. As an adventurer, she'd seen her fair share of armor shops, and this place had made some impressive replicas.

"Why not cheer on your favorite knight at the tournament wearing one of these?" said the stall owner, picking up one of the hats and showing how its visor could be moved up and down. "To be fair, there are no eyeholes, so you won't see much. Pull it down to your mouth and your whole head might stay warm, though."

"Wow!" said Priestess. She'd resolved not to spend frivolously, but she couldn't suppress a thrill just seeing it. Maybe it was the effect of the festival, of the joyous day.

The Earth Mother says to be frugal, but she doesn't say to not have fun.

Maybe she could buy just *one* hat…

"Oh!"

As she was looking, one helmet in particular caught her eye. Not because there was anything special about it. In fact, it looked like a helmet you might find anywhere…

"Looks a bit like Orcbolg's, doesn't it?"

"It sure does!"

High Elf Archer giggled, the sound like a bell jingling somewhere in her throat.

Well—as the expression went—since they'd come all this way. Maybe they should pick up a couple of these, too. The two of them laughed and nodded at each other.

"Pleasure doing business!" the shopkeeper said.

The hats cost several silver pieces each. During her days at the temple, Priestess could never have afforded it, but now she could.

And I even got a matching pair with my friend!

That thought alone was enough to make her heart dance.

"C'mon, let's wear 'em!"

"Er… Sure…"

She couldn't help feeling a touch of embarrassment at that suggestion. She was, after all, currently wearing her cleric's vestments. To trade her cap for a weird hat…

I feel like that might be enjoying myself a little too *much.*

She couldn't shake the sense—although she *did* want to put on her new hat.

"I think maybe…I'll wait and enjoy it during the big show."

"Aw, you don't have to be embarrassed!" High Elf Archer winked. She'd seen straight through Priestess.

The cleric looked at the headwear in her hands.

Well… I did come all this way…

To wear or not to wear? While the human was still deliberating, the elf was already moving. She somehow managed to squeeze her long ears into the woven hat.

"How do I look?!" she asked, her eyes sparkling.

"Like a very wonderful elf knight…at least from the neck up."

"Yeah, well, armor's so heavy. Ha! I'm no Orcbolg, you know!"

She did admit, however, that it pinched her ears a little bit. Then she set off in high spirits.

Noboru Kannatuki

Would this do for an offering? *That person* could be rather severe.

Ah, but…

If she'd been here now, she would certainly have been enjoying herself, hat or no hat. Priestess was sorry she couldn't have been, but the thought made her happy.

Then her musings were interrupted by a cry of "You there! Stop! You don't have to do that!"

She looked down the street and saw a frowning noblewoman rushing toward them. Priestess's eyes went wide, and she wondered what could be going on when she saw the woman reach for High Elf Archer's hat!

"H-hey, what do you think you're doing?!"

"You don't have to be embarrassed about being an elf! Don't hide your ears—let them stand proudly!" The woman's tone was sharp; she was as good as ordering High Elf Archer to take off the hat.

The noblewoman trundled up and made to grab High Elf Archer's new hat. Priestess quickly exclaimed, "S-stop that! What's the matter with you? She's not hiding anything—"

"And *you*!" The woman turned her glare on Priestess, pinning her in place. Priestess swallowed heavily but not from fear. She'd been subject to the gaze of more than one disgusting monster in her time, including one that was literally a giant eyeball. It was just… "A disciple of the Earth Mother, allowing this to happen! What's wrong with *you*, I must ask?!"

Surely there's no need to get so angry.…?

Priestess couldn't understand, and for a moment, she wasn't sure what to say. After she was finished dressing down the befuddled young cleric, the woman declared, "I'm going to lodge a complaint with your temple!" And then she stormed off with such force of will that the crowd parted before her as she went.

Still mystified, Priestess could only stand there. A complaint? She didn't even understand what the woman was angry about!

"Wh…what do you suppose that was all about?" she asked High Elf Archer.

"Search me. I'm not a big fan of dealing with people who are that upset anyway." The elf heaved a sigh, then her eyes met Priestess's. "It's…suffocating."

"Definitely."

The glum result of all this was that they found the wind taken out of their sails. They discovered they were no longer in the mood to put on new hats. High Elf Archer picked up the faux helmet that had been stripped off her head and ran her fingers through her hair to straighten it.

"Should we visit the graveyard now?" she asked.

"I guess so…," said Priestess.

They remembered the location from when they had visited last year, so there was no fear of getting lost. They bought flowers at a shop on the way, along with three encyti, a kind of fried treat. It consisted of a dough made of cheese and wheat squeezed through a funnel into a whirlpool shape, then fried in oil. Liberally flavored with honey and poppy seeds, it was aromatic and looked delicious.

"I think a girl ought to enjoy a treat like this," High Elf Archer said.

"Uh-huh," Priestess agreed. After a beat, she said, "I didn't get a chance to have dessert with her…"

"Well, hope she likes sweets. I'll bet she does."

I don't understand. Maybe it was the ruckus a few minutes earlier, but Priestess just couldn't feel lighthearted. Instead, she felt like she was sinking into a depression. In fact, she felt an ache in her neck. Why? And then…

"Wait… What?"

The graveyard proved to be another place where they discovered a most unusual sight. They stopped cold: Just beyond where the gravestones kept their silent vigil, there should have been statues of the gods. The five most venerated deities—the Earth Mother, the God of Knowledge, the Supreme God, the Trade God, and the Valkyrie. There should also have been two more statues enshrining the venerable gods that controlled Life and Death.

Yet they discovered that all the gods had been hidden under black cloths, to hide their likenesses.

"Something's up," said High Elf Archer. Priestess could only stand there flummoxed, but the elf was quicker. "Oh, hey! Hey, you!" She jogged over to a nearby cemetery visitor, her ears bouncing, and didn't wait for an invitation. "Why are those gods hidden?"

"Oh, that… Well, just think of all the different people who're here for the tournament." High Elf Archer was speaking to an old lady whose fingers brushed a gravestone engraved with a sword. Perhaps it belonged to a soldier. Her voice carried both annoyance and melancholy—certainly, there was no hint of pleasure in it. "There was an order given—those statues were to be covered in deference to visitors who don't worship these gods or follow other deities."

"I don't worship any particular god myself, but it never bothered me to have those statues here," High Elf Archer said.

"Well, those whom it *does* bother are louder than you, it would seem. A great pity." The woman shook her head slowly, then shuffled from the graveyard.

Priestess bowed to the old woman as she left and then to the grave the woman had been visiting. Beside the sword was carved a hammer, the sign of the Smithy God. These were people who strived to live well and uncover the secrets of steel.

"That was an odd conversation." High Elf Archer sniffed. She snorted, not very pleased by the situation, but then shrugged. "I guess it probably sounds good—the stuff about this graveyard and what that woman was saying earlier."

"I don't really understand myself," Priestess whispered disconsolately. Everything seemed darker to her, and she felt almost as if she were, yes, suffocating. Her neck felt downright sore now. Something like dust or ashes drifted through the air. She breathed in as best as her small chest would allow, then breathed out again. She didn't cough.

This is what Goblin Slayer would call…

…a town that felt like it was going to be attacked by goblins. The sense of Chaos. Some evil omen in the air.

And after we came all the way here for the tournament.

Would something really happen? Priestess had no answer. Would *she*, the wise and perceptive girl from Priestess's first party, have had one?

"Huh?" Priestess blinked as she took in the stone marking her friend's eternal slumber.

A single flower was already there, but she didn't know who could have left it.

§

"What?! You got rid of the rhea division?!" Rhea Fighter exclaimed. Wizard Boy frowned but managed not to say anything.

They were at the coliseum in the capital, which was big enough to dwarf anyone, even without reference to rheas. Eighty arched gates surrounded the place, each reaching a height of 160 feet, as tall and as imposing as a giant.

But this place was not called the coliseum, nor comparable to giants, simply because of its size. No, it was because in the past, there had been a massive statue called the Colossus outside it…

Or anyway, that was what Wizard Boy told Rhea Fighter, who kept begging him for factoids about the capital. Registration for tournament participants was taking place under one of the arches. The line was obscenely long, and while they waited, the girl pestered him endlessly with the question: "Hey, what's that?"

Still, it was better than being stared at as he stood there with a donkey wearing patchwork armor and its rhea minder. So he'd indulged her by answering—but when they had finally gotten to the front of the line, this was what they had found.

"Ah, orders from above, y'see…" Even the coliseum worker (who wore a wooden sword at his hip, evidence that he was a former competitor and victor himself) seemed bemused.

"So I can't be in the tournament?" Rhea Fighter asked.

"No, no, you can. But this year's tournament's to be held without divisions. Without discrimination, see."

"Discrimination?" Rhea Fighter said, as if the word was unfamiliar to her.

"I get it," Wizard Boy broke in. "So humans and rheas are going to be in the same group?"

"And elves and dwarves and padfoots and every other people you can think of."

"The hell? That hardly even makes sense."

"Sure doesn't." Rhea Fighter looked at Wizard Boy, her face full of questions. But oh well. If she could register, that was good enough. There wasn't an actual problem, as far as it went.

Having silently established this understanding, Rhea Fighter reached for the registration paperwork. Wizard Boy couldn't help thinking it might be better for him to fill it out, though, and went to take the pen from her…

"Huh! For all your vaunted learning, it looks like you still need a dose of enlightenment, Wizard."

A metal gauntlet reached out and stopped him.

"Guh?" The red-haired boy turned and glared at the interloper, who turned out to be a handsome man so tall Wizard Boy had to crane his neck to look at him. He wore pure-white armor (in the middle of town? Who did he think he was, *that guy*?) and was clearly a knight. The insignia of the sword and scales implied that he was perhaps one of the guardians of the halls of the Supreme God—a paladin.

"You can't assume she can't write just because she's a rhea. Go on, young lady. Go right ahead."

"Uh, no, I…," Rhea Fighter started before confessing in a mutter, "I don't write so well."

The knight held the pen out to her, but she only looked at the ground. Here was a handsome, obviously well-intentioned man trying to help her in front of a whole crowd of people. It was hard to say no to him. So with many an uneasy look at Wizard Boy, she began writing hesitantly in the register.

Her chicken-scratch scrawl stood out like a sore thumb among the names of the knights. It must have been humiliating.

"Do you understand now? Holding preconceptions about people based on their race is nothing but bias. Bias we must undo! In other words…" The knight seemed deeply gratified to see Rhea Fighter write her own name. He crossed his arms, *hmph*ed, and nodded. His eyes held Wizard Boy in place from well above the spellcaster's head. "We mustn't discriminate based on race nor think ourselves better than our fellow Pray-ers! We should all stand and compete side by side!"

"Uh…huh."

"It's called equality, boy. If we want an even playing field, where no one is persecuted and everyone can live comfortably, then equality is essential!"

Wizard Boy almost demanded what in the hell the knight was

talking about, but he managed to keep the words down. This wasn't the Sorcerers' Academy nor even the hut of that accursed old rhea. The man before him was no sage, and he wasn't that bastard "master." In other words, this wasn't a debate.

Hell, even if it was…

The guy was obviously completely uninterested in anything Wizard Boy might have to say, which didn't make for much of an argument. That much, Wizard Boy had learned from reflecting on his own past behavior.

"And you, young lady. You needn't force yourself to use a human sword. You can embrace rhea equipment without shame!"

"Huh?"

Rhea Fighter, however, reacted differently. The knight's gaze happened upon the large blade she carried. She, for one, responded with fury. Wizard Boy guessed she wouldn't be satisfied until she had chopped up the man in front of her.

Rheas didn't know much about politics. They were simple farmers who lived in their shire, smoking their tobacco and tending their fields. But this rhea was an adventurer now, and she was uncommonly sensitive to mockery. One of the things she'd learned from her grandfather who'd come back from deep under the mountain. She didn't care if she was dealing with a mad sorcerer or a soul-consuming necromancer.

I'll kill anyone who makes fun of me! That's being an adventurer.

The girl's eyes narrowed, and a cold light entered them. Her right hand was a blur as she grabbed the hilt of her sword.

Wizard Boy slapped his hand over hers before she could draw her weapon and exclaimed, "I understand what you mean, sir! I'll let your words inspire me as I seek to gain the knowledge I so sorely lack!"

He hoped his outburst would curtail the girl's moment of rage, and indeed, it took the wind clear out of her sails. He stood squarely in front of her, almost pressing her small body back. "But I think that's enough tutelage for today. We have more paperwork to do, and there are many people still waiting in line."

"Ah yes, of course. Mm! Very good, boy, let yourself be inspired. I take my leave!"

The knight in the white armor, once again looking quite satisfied about…well, *something*…turned on his heel with a click of his spurs. Rhea Fighter watched him stride away, growling like some frumious beast and staring daggers at him.

Barely a second later, she looked at Wizard Boy instead, and suddenly the attack turned on him. "Why'd you stop me?!"

"If you had started something here, *you* would've been the bad guy!"

"Who cares?! He was making fun of me! He said I shouldn't use a big sword, just 'cause I'm a rhea!" Wizard Boy could feel Rhea Fighter's chest, ample in spite of her small size, pressing against him as she raged.

Okay! Not the time for that!

He studiously forced its softness and size from his mind, searching desperately for the right words. To think of the bloodbath that would've ensued if things had gone sideways and the girl had drawn that oversized sword of hers…

"He's a knight. That means he'll probably be in this tournament. Take it out on him then," Wizard Boy said.

"You think he'll be there?!"

He hadn't exactly succeeded in talking her down, but he'd at least deflected the worst of her anger.

The rhea spun, her hair following her in a whirl. The coliseum attendant said, "Y-yes, I expect so… He's a fairly prominent knight in this city."

"Then he must have written his name down! Let me see it!"

If she can intimidate an accomplished swordsman, she might actually be able to take that guy down, Wizard Boy thought, finding himself impressed anew by his partner's guts. He looked over her shoulder at the register. The staff member pointed a grubby finger at one name out of the packed list of warriors.

"So that's him," Rhea Fighter growled.

"He's had some…pointed things to say. Not just about the tournament but the coliseum, too." The official sighed, sounding very put-upon. (The sigh seemed to be prompted by Rhea Fighter, who was staring at the name like the man had murdered her parents.) "It never used to be this way. The swordfighters were even grouped into divisions based on their fighting style."

Recently, the man lamented, it was hard to know what was happening. Things had just gotten so suffocating. People didn't mean any harm, but there was nothing you could say when someone accused you of being mistaken or even evil. (This was accompanied by another sigh.)

"Believe me, I sympathize," Wizard Boy muttered. The other man chuckled weakly.

"So which competition will the young lady be participating in?"

"Ah!" The boy held out his staff, tapping it against two of the shields that hung behind the official. One depicted knights jousting, the other a pair of crossed swords. Two different contests.

"Excellent. Good luck out there."

"Thanks."

As they walked away, they could hear the official saying, "Papers, please," to the next person in line.

Wizard Boy kept one eye on what was happening even as he bopped the rhea girl on the head with an open palm. "C'mon, let's get going. We're done with registration, and I don't want to be a part of any more commotions."

"Yeah...," was all Rhea Fighter said, but she nodded, took her donkey by the reins, and trotted off. Wizard Boy fell into step beside her, observing the crowds and general ruckus of the capital.

"Hey, don't worry about it," he said distantly, followed by: "I guess that won't stop you from worrying about it, will it?"

"Hell no."

"Figured." Wizard Boy nodded.

He had the same thought he'd had that morning, when they'd visited his older sister's grave before coming to the coliseum.

If only... If only.

If only the SOBs who had mocked his sister's death would appear at this moment, heads bowed in contrition—what would happen then? Would his rage abate even a little? He doubted it. The bastards might think that would make it all water under the bridge, but *he* would never believe that. He would never believe they had learned their lesson until he'd beaten them all to a pulp and cracked their heads open.

And of course, that was completely impossible. For one thing, his sister would give him a piece of her mind if he pulled something like that—even that awful old rhea would probably scoff at him. The moment he chose violence, the other guys would get to say they were the victims, and he would be the aggressor. It could only turn out bad for him.

But still…

There was a brief second when Wizard Boy thought he heard a voice he recognized, and he felt a tremor run through his body. He had to be imagining it. Hearing things. He was so focused on his thoughts that his mind must have been making things up.

That was what he told himself as he looked around—and spotted the robes of the Sorcerers' Academy.

It shouldn't have been surprising. This was the capital, and a tournament was afoot. Everyone would be there. Strangers and acquaintances alike.

Wizard Boy subconsciously picked up his pace, trying to put some distance between him and them. "If I get angry, I'll only get sucked into my own rage…," he insisted to himself.

"I just can't stand it!" Rhea Fighter said.

"Believe me, I know the feeling…"

He nodded again, then looked around the stalls and shops. Rheas ate five or six times a day. Maybe he could find a nice snack for her.

Times like this…

The important thing was to do something else, divert your train of thought. Human minds were very simple; they couldn't stay angry about something for long. He figured rheas were the same.

So why, then?

Why did the cityscape—the whole world—seem gray and ashen?

Now that he thought about it, he realized the armor worn by the man earlier had been the same. It had been of purest white, and yet to him it had seemed ashy.

The gray color overtook everyone around him; in his mind's eye, the whole town was daubed with it. The dead color of a burned-out fire.

"Hey, I was wondering." Wizard Boy's thoughts were interrupted by Rhea Fighter, who looked up at him from directly below. "What do you think that guy would do if a centaur or a giant wanted to be in the tournament?"

A centaur couldn't be knocked off their horse in a jousting match, and of course a giant would simply be too big to take part in any of the competitions. In those cases, it would be everyone else who would be at a disadvantage. The centaur and the giant probably wouldn't enjoy winning that way.

Or would they? The girl had no idea.

"Oh, I know what would happen." Wizard Boy snorted. "*Then* the guy would complain it was unfair!"

§

So passed another turbulent day in the capital.

Priestess and High Elf Archer appeared to have enjoyed their sight-seeing very much. The girl, his old friend, had had fun shopping and dining with Guild Girl. The shop that Dwarf Shaman and Lizard Priest had taken him to served food and drinks, although he hadn't understood very well what they were.

And as for me...

As the moments had carried him along until he was suddenly free, he found that he still didn't know what to do with a day off. He never had.

No...

He was outside the inn, the warmth of an unfamiliar alcohol filling the inside of his helmet and shielding him from the chill of the evening breeze. The lantern lights burned orange in the town, and he heard the burble of people passing by, the encroaching chatter.

Tomorrow was the tournament.

The night before, the town became a vast party, with people singing the praises of different knights and debating who would win. Even at the inn, the enthusiastic banter continued. High Elf Archer had taken Priestess, Guild Girl, and his old friend by the hand and dragged them to the tavern on the first floor. Lizard Priest and Dwarf Shaman were probably there as well. The women would be safe with them around.

As for him, he chose not to involve himself. He wasn't very good at living it up. Watching everyone else enjoy themselves, listening to their chatter—that, he thought, was ideal.

Nonetheless, here he was outside, watching the darkened streets of the capital.

No... It's hardly something new, this inability to imagine.

When had it started? Long, long ago, perhaps. The idea might already have been in his mind back when he had been asked to help with the dungeoneering contest. Had the seeds been planted in the desert, then?

Whatever the case, there was only one conclusion: *There is nothing besides goblin hunting.*

He'd gone to the desert in the east. The icy seas of the north. He'd met the centaurs of the grassy plains. Each of those experiences had made his heart race, he knew. And yet...he hadn't thought that was enough.

Nor did he now.

Here he was in the capital, observing the festivities. But he was not part of them. The thought caused him no anxiety, no dissatisfaction. He'd simply found that he was not part of that circle.

So when a voice asked, "Clearing your head?" he was, for a moment, unsure how to react. Who would bother speaking to a man standing by the entrance of an inn, observing the celebrations?

With some effort, he turned his helmeted head and found Guild Girl standing there. Her cheeks were slightly flushed.

"Yes, I am," he said. It was the only answer he could think of. "I believe I am."

"Oh, you are?"

"Yes."

Guild Girl giggled at that, but he didn't know why. Had he said something funny?

Then she walked up beside him and, regardless of any lack of decorum, plopped herself down by the roadside. This was not the conduct of a refined young lady. Neither the Guild nor the nobility would approve of such behavior.

Goblin Slayer looked at the night cityscape as if it might tell him what to say.

"…Your home," he offered at length. *Yes. It must be here.* Goblin Slayer's avowedly slow mind finally dredged the fact up out of his memory. "Is it all right if you don't go to say hello?"

"My! Would you be so kind as to go with me?" Guild Girl replied, and her expression was teasing. She added, "That's a joke," before he could answer. "Anyway… I think it's all right. At least, as far as I'm concerned."

"…I see."

"Yes. It's not that we don't get along, but…I think going home would only earn me a stern talking-to."

Goblin Slayer didn't think anything in particular about that. He simply recognized that this was how it was for her.

He had only about ten years' experience with families. He knew no more of them than that.

Guild Girl, though, appeared somehow embarrassed. Perhaps she thought of it as an indulgence.

"Hey," she said. "Want to take a walk?"

Goblin Slayer had no particular reason to refuse.

No…

He corrected himself: He *personally* had no reason.

"If you'll have me," he said.

"Well, that's why I invited you." Guild Girl puffed out her cheeks a little.

Confronted with that, Goblin Slayer could only say: "I see."

That answer seemed to satisfy Guild Girl, who stood up, shaking out her long, slim legs. She smiled into the night and said, "Let's go!"

The lanterns of the city, lit by students from the Academy, gave off a magical light, illuminating Guild Girl's face in profile. Goblin Slayer suspected the same light played off the cheap armor beside her.

I'm walking along with someone.

Through an unfamiliar cityscape. A place he had never dreamed he would see. Yet now he was visiting the capital for the second time.

It was the strangest thing. His sister would have been much better suited to this place than he was. The fact that he was here felt wrong to him. Yet at the same time, he noticed…

"People aren't looking at me so much."

"It's a big town," Guild Girl said. "And there's a festival to boot."

To her, those reasons explained it all.

There they were, a daughter of the nobility dressed to the nines, accompanied by a slayer of goblins in grimy armor.

But no one seems to care.

He wondered if that could actually be true.

Guild Girl said nothing.

For a long moment, neither did he.

"…"

"……"

"……Yah!" she exclaimed as she flung herself against him, grabbing his arm.

"Hrm…," he grunted. She'd caught him by surprise.

Filthy metal was pressed into the chest of her unsullied blouse. The softness and warmth didn't reach him. Only the pressure. She felt heavier, more *present*, than the shield he forever had tied to his arm. But he would be more careful with her than he was with his shield.

She'll get dirty. The thought was something close to worried.

"I'm filthy," he said. "You'll get dirty."

"I don't mind." Clutching his armored arm, Guild Girl gazed forward, smiling triumphantly. "How long do you think I've known you?"

"I see…"

"I'll bet you do!"

Argh! I can't believe this guy!

Guild Girl might not have known him as long as his childhood friend, but it had been some years by this point. She might not know or notice everything about him, but watching him now, there were plenty of things she did understand.

He was an accomplished adventurer of the Silver rank. It was a tremendous achievement, and he was very well regarded.

And I'm not sure if he knows it.

Probably not, she figured. Not to suggest that was why she liked him so much.

I've chosen to be happy, all on my own. Whatever he might think of himself, I can't do anything about it, but it doesn't matter. I've fostered my own feelings over years and years. This is my life. No one else has a say in it—not even him. I'll be happy if I choose to be. I don't need anyone else to do anything for me to make me that way. So…sure. Why not a little love? Surely this much…

"…This much I can be allowed, right?"

"If that's what you want…," he began.

Goblin Slayer thought: *What a boring thing to say. A silly thing.* Was that all he could say to her? Had he no more substance than that? He grew more and more annoyed with himself. All the years they had grown closer, all the years she had watched out for him and helped him, and that was all he could muster for her?

"…then it's all right."

"It is!"

They spent a few moments observing the bustle of the capital. Walking with no particular destination, chatting about nothing in particular, window-shopping at the stalls, watching people go by, until they came back to the inn.

It was no more of a night than that. And no less.

"What in the world are you thinking, Your Majesty?!"

There was a smack of an open palm hitting the tabletop, and the various members of the royal council frowned at one another as if to say: *This again?* The expression was out of place on the faces of clerics who were administering a tournament held in offering to the many and great deities.

The one who had raised his voice was a handsome knight of the Supreme God's halls, his neck bedecked with the symbol of his deity.

This youth had been full of fervor for the running of the tournament, and no one necessarily resented him for it. Young men ought to burn with passion for their ideals. If he was striving to overcome challenges and obstacles, for that matter, why not help him?

But this was going too far.

"Using Sense Lie upon our visitors from the underground empire? That's discrimination against dark elves!"

How many times was this now?

Not just how many times across the course of the council's meetings, although there was that. This was the fifth time *today*.

He was testing the patience of the various representatives who had come on behalf of their temples. Only the young king showed no sign of fatigue in the face of the stalled meeting. He merely replied, "I'm not saying dark elves are evil. Only that there's a possibility of spies coming from the underground empire."

"Please don't try to talk past this, sir!"

You're the one talking past things! thought King's Sister, who for reasons mysterious to her had been made the representative from the Temple of the Earth Mother. She fought back a yawn.

Dark elves weren't evil? Sure, anyone with a bit of education knew that. Ever since the legendary dark elf ranger had first blazed the path, decent dark elves had been plentiful in the Four-Cornered World. But that had no bearing on the threat posed by the dark elves' underground empire. They were biding their time, looking for any chance to strike.

Thus it was the underground empire that was dangerous, not dark elves. Even a child could understand that.

"I must say, you seem to be suggesting that we shouldn't allow dark elves in the tournament at all," King said.

"Only because at this moment, it would be as good as putting them in the stocks for public ridicule! It would be discourteous to allow them to appear on the grounds under the circumstances!"

Wouldn't that be exactly the opposite of what you're actually saying, then? King's Sister thought disinterestedly. She uttered, "Hrmf" as she only half managed to stifle the next yawn. *They say dark elves are just as gorgeous as other elves...*

For better or for worse, she had yet to meet one herself. She'd only ever seen them in picture books. They had skin as dark as night and lithe bodies that reminded her of predatory animals.

During some unpleasant events that she mostly preferred not to remember, King's Sister had gained a friend from among the ancient high elves. She seemed as lovely and delicate as a fairy, her beauty at once like and deeply unlike that of the dark elves.

Oh, but...

She seemed to remember a female elf in the frontier town, the one where the dungeoneering contest had been held, who had been hard-edged and lean. She'd caught a glimpse of her arguing with a female wizard about something.

That was what it came down to. Your race was just something

you were born with, another starting stat. She could obviously agree that dark elves weren't inherently evil. That was a laudable thing to think.

But at the rate he's going, this knight is going to end up arguing that the underground empire itself isn't even evil!

Dark elves aren't evil, so their underground empire can't possibly be, the argument would go. Not that dark elves themselves would probably give a flying fig what humans made of their history. They were undying people who hailed from the Age of the Gods. They were different from short-lived humans in every way.

"We need to join hands with the dark elves and live in harmony. You must understand that!" the knight was saying.

"I do, and I have no objection to that statement," King replied.

Despite the vast gulf between humans and dark elves, this young paladin insisted on getting into a shouting match over every little point. "*This is wrong, that has to be corrected*"—always in the name of justice. It started to wear very thin after a while.

King's Sister was growing tired of just sitting and listening. Besides, at this point, the meeting would never be over. So she marshaled her resolve and, in an attempt to get a word in edgewise amid the tirade taking place under the guise of reasonable argument, said, "Um…"

The paladin rounded on her, his eyes still blazing with righteous indignation.

"Erk!" King's Sister said. But she couldn't let herself be silenced now.

I'm not scared of him.

At least, he wasn't any more frightening than the goblins in the Dungeon of the Dead or the lumps of flesh she'd encountered beneath the frontier town. All right, so maybe it wasn't very "polite" to compare him to those things!

"There's something I'd like to ask on behalf of several of the temples here." Yes, something to ask. She coughed sweetly, then screwed up her courage and said, "Why do you feel the images of the Earth Mother need to have their wings covered?"

"The Earth Mother is our god, not that of the birdfolk. It's disrespectful to them to put wings on her."

"It's what?" King's Sister blurted out before she could stop herself.

I don't think I've ever heard anyone say that…

Fair enough; maybe there were people who didn't like it. But then there were also plenty of birdfolk who followed the Earth Mother. The paladin said "our," apparently meaning humans, but the Earth Mother didn't belong to humans alone. King's Sister was so confused she felt like there must have been a question mark floating over her head.

"If it's a matter of respect," she said, "I should think hiding or painting over the wings is far more disrespectful…"

"May I take it, then, that the Temple of the Earth Mother has no interest in being considerate of the birdfolk?"

"No, you may not." She was about to add that wasn't the issue, but she swallowed the words.

Now the paladin appeared to take this as agreement (how convenient). He gesticulated vigorously, as if delivering a real lecture, and continued loudly: "The clergy are altogether too unmindful! Consider the disgraceful outfits worn for the performance at the opening ceremony!"

"You dare refer to our deity's battle vestments as disgraceful…?! Unbelievable!"

This cry came from a young half-elf woman, a cleric of the Valkyrie. She wore armor that looked more like underwear beneath an outer garment of sheer silk, and she was present on behalf of the chief cleric of the Valkyrie's temple. Word was that she used to be an adventurer, or perhaps still was, and that some of those standing guard outside the room she counted among her friends.

King's Sister heaved a sigh, having at least escaped the paladin's immediate attention. She leaned back in her chair. She was sweating and so, so tired.

"They show a lack of respect toward women. Are they not the outfits of gladiators? Truly, a symbol of barbarity."

"They are a sign that anyone can rise to sit with our god, even if they began as a slave!"

However, the paladin (was he really a servant of the Supreme God? King's Sister couldn't believe it) continued to expound. "The whole problem is that we have so many stories lauding slaves! Take the barbarian king in the north..."

Oops! Good thing she's *not here,* King's Sister thought. The letter she'd received from her friend recently had been full of praise for the warriors of the north.

"The saga of a man who kills and rapes and conquers territory, all in order to become king? Such base material should be thrown out like the trash it is."

"That's ridiculous!" A slow sigh came from the young woman present on behalf of the temple of the God of Knowledge. "Is that how you see those heroic tales? As nothing but praise of murder and violation?"

"It's wrong to disseminate materials so readily susceptible to such interpretations..."

"Those stories were born in a land that worships the Smithy God and the sadistic god. They come from a worldview with a completely different outlook on violence from ours."

At the calm young woman's feet, King's Sister caught glimpses of a strange white creature. It met her gaze, and of all things, it winked and pressed its forepaws to its mouth.

Don't worry... I won't say anything.

It seemed all too clear that if she did, it would only set the paladin off afresh.

"Say what you will, but their land is an ally of our kingdom now. They're going to have to reform their thinking."

"So you place limits on knowledge and culture and go back in history to pass judgment on the past? You must be a far greater being than I can even imagine. How hopeless." The young woman, beloved of the God of Knowledge, shook her head, and King's Sister nodded along. She couldn't have agreed more, from the bottom of her heart.

"Perhaps I might offer a word?" came a firm voice from the cleric of the Trade God, who had been watching silently until that moment. A silver-haired woman with eyes like ice, she raised her hand to speak with a glance around the table. "There are, in fact, *many* words I would like to offer, but I shall start with one."

King's Sister caught sight of her brother, who smirked and nodded.

Does he know her?

It was possible. The woman was absolutely lovely, but King's Sister couldn't seem to recall having seen her before. She almost felt like the wind, as if she might slip past and disappear as easily as she came.

"You said that we should cease paying salaries to the padfoots, because this is not a zoo, did you not?"

"I did indeed!" the paladin said, bursting with fresh zeal. "Observe the costumes servers wear in the gambling dens—modeled after hare-folk! If that's not exploitation, I don't know what is!"

"Many enjoy dressing that way. It makes things livelier, and it keeps the silver flowing. Which I *certainly* appreciate."

The paladin's expression took on a contemptuous cast. The young woman's even smile never faltered, however, as she continued: "And what do you propose to do about all the padfoots your policy would put out of a job?"

"They can find any kind of work they like! Such is freedom!"

"You seem to think that money and employment are things that arise like clouds or mist." The woman snorted, a sound of derision. "But you know, even the wind does not come from nothing."

Ignoring the paladin's nonplussed look, the cleric of the Trade God adjusted her spot in her chair. Somehow, she made it look elegant. Then she held out an open palm as if to say, *Please, continue.* The paladin of the Supreme God growled.

If King's Sister had been in his place, she would have been very nearly lost for words. Such, however, was not this man's problem. "Race itself—race itself is a bizarre idea. Are we not all people alike? All should be treated as humans and—"

Oops. Here it comes.

"At this rate, I feel like you're going to say *I* should be succeeded by a woman."

"Erk…"

The paladin almost choked at the unexpected remark from behind him, delivered in a low, silky murmur. He glanced back to find a man standing like a shadow, a man of vigilant mien wearing a tuxedo whose every line and angle seemed to fit him precisely. One might describe him as like a butler, but no butler had the shocking self-possession of the figure standing there.

To King's Sister, who knew who he was and what he did, it all seemed a little much.

"...Aren't you looking a bit *too* nice for the occasion?" she said.

"I'm good enough to get away with dressing like this."

The silver-haired woman seated behind King gave the man a sharp look that seemed to contain a warning: *Don't bait the king's younger sister.* Of course, this woman had a less-than-expressive face, but even King's Sister could read what she was thinking from time to time.

"Oops, the boss is angry. And here I just rushed back from the water town as fast as I could."

"Your efforts are appreciated, I'm sure."

"I didn't even sleep on the job!"

No doubt he'd started at least one fight big enough to fuel a good story or three.

With a motion so smooth nobody noticed it start—well, perhaps the cleric of the Trade God did?—the flashy man stepped forward, most likely to report to King.

King's Sister didn't have to think to know who this man was, whose face was different each and every time they met.

"...Ahhh..."

At the umpteenth sense that she was going to yawn, she finally decided to let it out. She was so very tired. Her body was heavy and her head felt dull. She was hot all the way through, until she suddenly got cold.

I'm exhausted...

Yes, that had to be it. How could she not be, with the discussion going in circles around her for so long?

So King's Sister dismissed the fatigue she was feeling and forgot about it. She had no idea how much longer the attendees at this meeting were going to continue their little dance.

She thought, though, that she caught a smell—a terrible odor of ash.

CHAPTER 2

They Call Me

This—*this* was what it meant for the air to be full of passion.

Spectator seats towered over the circular field of battle, covered with tents to keep the sun off. There must have been room for ninety thousand people. The seats had been arranged with careful calculation and planning such that the contests would be visible from every one of them. No one had reason to complain, no matter where they were seated. Indeed, instead they would be thanking the Trade God if they had the good fortune to purchase a tessera, an entry ticket.

Out of the eighty rounded arches, no fewer than seventy-six were allocated for spectator use. Each tessera had a number from 1 to 76, indicating the gate through which the spectator was to enter. Row and seat numbers were also given, leading each person directly to their seat.

Guests sat on the provided cushions, bought snacks from the sellers who worked the rows, and waited with barely contained excitement for the spectacle to begin. They were watching a circular field of combat covered in white sand. Here, swordfighters competed against one another daily, no quarter asked and none given, all in offering to the Valkyrie, who, legend told, had fought once here herself a very long time ago.

Admittedly, the statue of the Valkyrie had recently come under serious criticism—but today of all days, there would be no questions. The statue of the Valkyrie stood proudly uncovered, watching over the battlefield.

Hoh! May the Valkyrie see the deeds that are done!

But it was more than the exterior accoutrements of the coliseum that deserved attention. The bowl at the bottom, believe it or not, could be filled with water to stage naval battles. It had been said this would no longer be possible after the construction of underground passageways, greenrooms, and even an elevator. But the engineering capabilities of the dwarves, who could make it so not a single drop escaped, were something to behold! They worked the stone with their exceptional abilities, renovating the coliseum while maintaining all the equipment. If facing and overcoming seemingly impossible obstacles was the essence of worship of the Valkyrie, then those dwarves were faithful warriors in their own right.

And now today, another such warrior, a young woman, was in the underground passageway.

"Ah... Ahhh... I th-think I'm suddenly having an attack of nerves..."

Shaking violently, equipped with hand-me-down armor and sitting on a donkey, was a rhea girl. The jousting spear she'd been given looked almost comically large compared to her tiny body. She held it easily, though, even considering that it was a lightened wooden instrument designed to shatter.

"Don't tell me you're getting cold feet," said the boy holding the donkey's reins with a glance at his partner. He could look her right in the face, because she had her visor up—maybe she felt a bit suffocated keeping it down, what with the cotton padding and a heavy metal helmet over that.

Her teeth were gritted like she was trying to control herself, and her eyes flicked back and forth. "I'm n-n-not. I just c-can't get my body to stop shaking!"

"That's a good sign." He prevented himself from adding the words that flitted through his mind: *I think*. Instead, he patted her lightly on the thigh. He could never have done it if she hadn't been wearing armor—or if they hadn't been in exactly the position they were.

He wasn't used to spending all his time, waking and sleeping, with a girl his own age. (Well, technically, their ages were very different.) It was nothing like being with his older sister.

"Your body and your brain can each be doing their own thing. Your body's just getting ready to fight," he said.

"Y-you think so…?"

He was only repeating something he'd heard, but the rhea girl clung to it for dear life.

In fact, he suspected, it was as simple as this: The moment was upon them, and she was scared. He didn't let that ugly thought onto his tongue but instead swallowed it down. She didn't need quibbling explanations—over the years, he'd learned that much.

"Yeah. It's like…doing warm-up exercises. You should move a little yourself."

"Oh… Yeah, you're right." She actually listened to him, twisting in her saddle and shaking herself out as best she could. Her armor clanked as she moved, and then she looked at him again, worried. "I'm not sure I can raise my shoulders…"

"Well, why would you need to do that for a joust?"

Thus, Wizard Boy cut straight through her fears. Anxiety was words; namely, a spell. Words didn't have to be words of *true* power to have power nonetheless.

"Just make sure you stretch them out before the sword fight, and you'll be fine."

"R-right…!"

Not long after, the fight before theirs must've ended, because there was a huge cheer from the hallway, in the direction of the light of the battlefield. Wizard Boy could sense the rhea girl taking deep breaths. He patted her back gently. She nodded: *Right.* The hand holding her lance moved to lower her visor.

"If you please, it's your turn," said a woman who wore armor covering only the most *essential* places. She was one of the clerics of the Valkyrie, distinguished warriors who believed that so long as their vital parts were covered, they could take care of everything else themselves. "I wish you good luck in your battle!"

"Mm! Thanks," Rhea Fighter replied with as much conviction as she could. Her helmet was fastened in place with another *clank*, and then she let out a breath. "Let's go!"

"You got it."

Wizard Boy tugged on the donkey's reins and started forward. The animal began to move, the clop of hooves echoing in the hall. As they approached, the light of the battlefield seemed to get bigger, stronger, until it filled their entire field of vision with white...

"Oh, wow...!" the girl exclaimed at the deafening cheers that rained down on them from every side.

They were not, however, cheers of welcome for her. The crowd was simply thrilled to see another battle. If one of the contestants was a little girl far smaller than any of them had expected, so much the better. Maybe she would go flying in spectacular fashion—or otherwise show her tenacity. That was what flourished among those spectators: a heartless disinterest in the rhea, a certainty that she could be nothing special.

"Uh... Ah..." Rhea Fighter clenched her teeth, which threatened to chatter loud enough to be heard through her armor. *I shouldn't have come*, she thought. She didn't belong here. She would only embarrass herself. She should quit now.

She had heard those words and others like them leveled against her many times in the past. She'd always fought back, but now they swirled in her head. She'd thought she had chased them away long ago, but here they were, pressing in, threatening to crush her.

After all, just look: Look at her opponent, the knight standing at the far end of the two parallel tracks of the field. The heavy armor. The warhorse on which he sat. The plethora of decorations to be expected at a jousting tournament.

Those decorations alone set the opponent apart from her at that moment. And the servant who stood by the knight was dressed like the very picture of nobility. The rhea girl was not familiar with the station known as a herald. Or at least, she hadn't been until her partner, the boy, had volunteered to be hers. As a result, when confronted with a real knight and a real herald, she was at a loss for what to do.

The herald unrolled a scroll and began to recite his master's family history at a clip:

"*Ahem!* Before you stands a knight of the plains of the four corners. His father distinguished himself doing battle against the Death, while his grandfather…"

The litany of achievements went on for a full six generations into the past. The rhea girl, of course, had nothing of the sort. She hardly even followed what the herald was saying. Thus she could only assume it was somehow her fault that the audience had suddenly fallen quiet.

She flinched when she heard a whisper from beside her: "What a shit herald."

It was Wizard Boy. She looked at him, her helmet clanking as she did so, but he said only, "Just watch me," and stepped forward.

No, in fact, he said more than that—Rhea Fighter noticed him intoning the words of the Magnify spell.

"*Before you,*" he boomed, "*is the finest fighter known in the shire of the rheas!*"

His voice shook the very air, resounding like thunder. The chattering spectators summarily shut up.

There was an instant of calm, of silence. Then, with a great wave of his arm, Wizard Boy said as if he had sucked in all the air in the stadium:

"*Her first mentor was the renowned adventurer, he who went there and back again deep under the mountain, the great swordmaster of the rheas!*"

He actually remembered it! The rhea girl found her eyes going wide under her helmet.

It was an old story, of which she told him only bits and pieces. She didn't despise the shire, but it held few happy memories for her. Her eccentric and somewhat off-kilter grandfather had taught her to use a sword, forcing her to practice until she nearly collapsed.

That was how it had all started. If the old man hadn't taught her the blade, she wouldn't have been here now.

"*Day and night, she trained, a thousand days spent learning, ten thousand more refining her craft—and now she stands before you!*"

*　　*　　*

She couldn't help smiling at that. She wanted to object that she wasn't *that* old.

That was all it took to get her quivering chin to relax. The feeling soon spread to the rest of her body.

"Her strikes fall like lightning upon the enemy! I urge you, watch what she does!"

The young man bowed elegantly. There was the briefest of beats, and then the stadium erupted in cheers. Even then, they weren't for the rhea girl. Their cries consisted of simple passion, excitement at the prospect that things might turn out more interesting than anticipated.

And yet for the girl, they felt very different. As the boy came back, his breath heaving, she gripped his sleeve with one gauntleted hand and said, "Hey, where'd you learn to do that?"

"From the old guy," he said, apparently meaning their master. "He told me a wizard needs something to impress at the right moment." He didn't sound very appreciative. Finally, he gave her another gentle slap on the back. "Eyes front. Don't forget what I said."

"R-right…!" The rhea girl took several deep breaths, then took the donkey's reins and urged the animal forward.

This was nothing like where she'd fought in the shire. This was a proper jousting field. The other end looked so far away, and there her opponent sparkled in the sunlight, acting as if the match was already won.

Or—no. Was that just her imagination, her assumption? She wasn't sure. But it didn't matter.

That's right. My strikes are like lightning.

The judge gave a great wave of his flag. The rhea gave her donkey the spurs.

"Y-yaaaahhh…!"

"Hrrrrahhhh!"

She felt as if time was running slowly, the air fighting her as though she was underwater. Her vision narrowed until all she could see was her opponent.

She raised her right hand. She had to couch the lance. No. There—there it was. No!

"Listen."

It was something the boy had said to her over and over as they made their way here. Now, at this moment, it came tumbling out from the storehouse of her memories.

"Power is simple logic. It's made up of three things: speed, weight, and force."

That and transmission. *"So four things,"* he'd muttered.

"This transmission, it has three parts. The fulcrum, the point of action, and the point where the force is applied."

"I don't know what you're talking about. It doesn't make any sense to me." She could listen as hard as she wanted; some things still just wouldn't click.

"You're gonna lose out on body size, so that already puts you at a disadvantage. And you can't put out a lot of force. I mean, that's just a fact."

"Uh-huh." The girl had nodded dejectedly. She was all too aware of the difference in size. And she couldn't shake the thought that calculating advantage and disadvantage before a fight was the sort of thing that only a coward would do. But the boy, he was telling her how to win. So she'd nodded along. She'd listened to him.

"Speed, the opponent will provide. Which means all that's left is transmission."

"So what do I do?"

"Stay on your mount. Don't take the blow head-on. Keep a firm hold on your lance, and make sure you stick it in the right place."

She felt the lance click neatly into the metal rest as everything came together.

The rhea leaned forward as far as she could. It was very uncomfortable on her chest, which was squeezed by her chest plate.

Overhead, something grazed the top of her helmet, scraping along. She heard wood splintering. A shock. She was shaken violently.

Don't think about it.

Then with a great shout, "Kiiieeeehhhhh…!!" she brought her spear up with all the force of a burning brushfire. Her right arm felt like she'd struck a brick wall; it went numb with the impact, while the tip of her spear splintered and went everywhere.

The flow of time spontaneously caught up to her.

Air came rushing back into her lungs like she'd broken through the surface of the water, and there was noise everywhere.

"Haaah…!" Inside her suffocating helmet, she gasped like a fish thrown onto dry land.

There was no time to rest, however. Burgeoning panic was all she could feel as the blood rushed to her brain.

"The sword contest!" she shouted and leaped down from her donkey. The heavy armor caused her to lean vertiginously as she landed. Or was that the lack of oxygen? She wasn't sure.

Just as she thought she would tilt clean over, she felt a lean arm grab her from one side and hold her up.

"My armor! Fix my armor, quick! The shoulders—!"

"Calm down." With a *clank*, her helmet was removed, and then someone grabbed the padding beneath and tore it away. She felt the wind hit her sweat-soaked cheeks and forehead.

"Phew!" she breathed. "I—I *am* calm! But there's no time to—"

"I told you, calm down. Eyes front."

"Wha—?"

She looked where she was bidden and discovered her opponent flat on his back. In fact, his helmet was rolling across the field, clanking as it went. The herald rushed over and splashed him with water but to no avail.

"You knocked him out in one blow," the boy said with a grin, and finally the girl came back to herself.

She also noticed that every eye in the coliseum was on her.

That produced an *urk*. It gave rise to an *eep*. Hesitation, embarrassment, excitement, and confusion.

Amid the swirl of emotions, the girl felt the boy take her hand, his grip strong for such a slim arm, and hold it aloft. The tight shoulders of her armor miraculously accommodated the motion. She looked up in amazement, the audience filling her vision.

"Behold! The Sting of the rheas! The blow that can bury even a spider in the dark!"

Another cheer rent the stadium air, and this time, it was for her.

§

"Oh my gosh! She did it! She won!"

"Mm."

Priestess clapped her hands with innocent joy, while Goblin Slayer crossed his arms and simply nodded. Only a few people in the stands were not participating in the thunderous cheering, and his section was one of them.

They were sitting in a private box rather more well-appointed than the general spectator seating. Priestess, High Elf Archer, Guild Girl, and even Cow Girl had been rooting for a victory by their acquaintance the entire time.

"I sure never expected to see those two here!" High Elf Archer said, clapping her hands and adding that they'd become quite a team.

"Mm," Goblin Slayer said and nodded again.

The elf giggled with a sound like a tinkling bell. "That's all we ever get from you, isn't it, Orcbolg?"

"Is that so?"

"Sure is."

But, well, it wasn't such a bad thing, High Elf Archer concluded, smiling innocently.

The boy and girl down there were two of the rare people—or perhaps it wasn't so rare after all?—that Goblin Slayer had looked after and helped. High Elf Archer didn't know much about honor and glory in the human world, but winning at a tournament had to be a good thing.

And Orcbolg wouldn't know how to just openly congratulate somebody like our friend there.

If the man in the grimy armor were to suddenly launch into a panegyric to her performance, even the high elf would have to be shocked.

Having reached this conclusion, High Elf Archer promptly turned her attention to other things. For there were so many things to be interested in. For example…

"They said it was a best-of-three contest, but she hit him in the head and knocked him off his horse, so she wins, right?" Yes, for example, the precise rules of this jousting tournament that had everyone so excited. She twirled her raised pointer finger, directing her questions at the bulky man beside her. "How would they decide who won if nobody fell off their horse?"

"Hmm. You saw the lances splinter, I presume?" Lizard Priest said with much gravity.

"Sure did. They both went, like, *bam!* and vaporized!"

"The shattering of the lance indicates a direct hit. Thus, the one with the shattered lance would be awarded a point."

If nobody was unhorsed, then destroying your lance earned you a point. If you both managed it—or if you both didn't—then it was a draw. Of course, sometimes both parties were knocked off their mounts, or they went three rounds equal on points.

"If there is to be a sword contest, then the crossing of lances does not conclude matters."

Ah, how wonderful was this legalized form of mock combat!

High Elf Archer nodded, trying to ignore the tickle of Lizard Priest's tail wrapping itself around her leg.

"Those aren't real lances, though, right?" she said. "They're designed to break. Doesn't that make them pretty fragile?"

"Yes, they're fragile," said Dwarf Shaman. "Which makes 'em a mite easier on an armored body."

The dwarf always had a word to say about weaponry. Get a dwarf started on either alcohol or smithing, and he was unlikely to stop.

He informed them that it was equivalent to the force of a "gunshot."

More, he added, there was once a king who had been killed by a flying splinter.

"Huh," was all High Elf Archer had to offer to such trivia. She started looking around again. "So that's why they wear all that armor. I thought it was just humans, you know, preening for one another."

"It's true, their equipment certainly is *bright* and *shiny*," replied Priestess, with a sidelong glance at the adventurer in the filthy, cheap-looking suit of armor beside her. He still had his arms crossed and was looking at the pair on the battlefield far below, the boy holding up the girl's hand, and nodding in what seemed to be satisfaction.

They're so different, Priestess found herself thinking, but she didn't mean it critically. Her party leader was this somewhat odd adventurer, and she had no objections to that.

"If someone is unhorsed but takes their mount down with them, it's considered to be the horse's fault, and the knight doesn't lose. The match is annulled," Guild Girl said, adding with some hesitation that if the rider is knocked unconscious, it's all over anyway.

Yes—with some hesitation. That provoked Cow Girl's curiosity. It seemed *she* and *he* had been on a walk the night before, just the two of them...

But hey.

She felt she could take that to mean that this evening, it would be her turn. She'd been in a good mood ever since that morning. It was the day of the long-awaited tournament. She could wear the outfit she'd bought yesterday. A perfect excuse to get dressed up—and it had earned her the assessment "*It looks good on you...I believe.*"

"You look pretty pleased," Cow Girl said. He did, in fact, seem extraordinarily satisfied and that made her happier than anything. She slid over to him and looked down at him, into the visor of his helmet.

"Hmm...," she heard, as if he was having trouble parsing the meaning of her words.

She found that indescribably amusing and fought to keep herself from grinning openly.

"Those two—they won!" she said. Weren't they his protégés? Well, of course they won.

"Hrm...," was his response. He looked at the ground, was quiet for a moment, and then murmured, "I see... Yes, that's true." He suspected he was—he confirmed with a nod—happy.

That was unlikely to be simply because Wizard Boy and Rhea Fighter had been victorious. When they had left their homes, traveling all the way to the town on the frontier, they had been just two among many adventurers. But they had made their way out into the world, and now here they stood, with the eyes of the whole capital upon them. That fact, she was sure, must make him happy.

And you're Silver-ranked yourself!

Cow Girl didn't know much about adventurers' ranks, but she knew you didn't reach Silver by accident.

"Hey, why didn't any of the other Silver-ranked people come out for this? You know, the guy with the spear or the guy with the big sword?"

"Ahhh, them?" Guild Girl said, not expecting the question. "They don't have much interest in things like this…" She trailed off.

Strange. This all sounded familiar to Cow Girl, but…not quite.

Hmm? She turned and looked and caught a glimpse of Earth Mother vestments. For a second, she thought maybe Priestess had asked the question—but no. This girl's frame, the length of her hair, and her facial expression all resembled Priestess but only superficially.

Her eyes met Cow Girl's, and the smile she gave her was like the sun coming out from behind the clouds. "Sorry to drop in!" the girl chirped.

"Y-Your Highness?!" There was a shuffle as Guild Girl abruptly straightened up.

"Highness?" Cow Girl said, cocking her head.

Guild Girl was still flustered. "Wh-when did you get here?! Uh, er, please excuse my rudeness…"

"It's all right, really. I snuck in. Or snuck out, I guess."

The king's little sister (Cow Girl didn't know that's who she was) laughed out loud and waved away Guild Girl's concern. She had a puckish twinkle in her eye, which soon settled on the girl who looked so much like her. "It's been a while. Have you been well?"

"Yes!" Priestess replied, and her smile was like a blossoming flower.

They definitely look like each other, but…not exactly.

Even two girls who looked virtually identical were clearly distinguishable if you knew at least one of them. But in any case, more women meant more chatter—and more loveliness.

Above all, no one in the booth objected to the addition of another friend.

Lizard Priest slid his massive body over, High Elf Archer pressing in as well, to make a space into which the new girl slipped. Guild Girl shifted, evidently feeling awkward about something, but Dwarf Shaman laughed jovially. "What's this, then, Princess?" (Cow Girl cocked her head again: Princess?) "A bit o' hooky, eh?"

"That's right. I couldn't stand another minute of that meeting; it just wouldn't end! So I showed myself out." She stuck out her tongue playfully; Guild Girl placed her hands on her stomach and tried to restrain a smile.

Huh?

Priestess blinked as she observed the scene. Her color was poor—not the receptionist's, the king's little sister. She was paler than Priestess, of course, and her skin looked dewy enough, but it was more than that. It looked like her circulation was weak—maybe like she was tired—or then again, maybe not quite.

"Um, are you okay...?" Priestess asked. It was a natural question. She felt a twinge at the back of her neck, a bad feeling she couldn't seem to shake.

"Yeah, I'm fine. Doing great. I think I'm just a little tired," King's Sister replied.

For her part, High Elf Archer seemed bothered as well—or maybe it was pangs of sympathy since her social position was much like this girl's. She peered into King's Sister's face, then said in a chiding tone, "I know human lives are short, but you don't have to hurry around quite *that* much!"

"If only we could all measure things the same way the elves do!" King's Sister laughed. She abruptly slouched over.

And then, almost before the others could register what was happening, her delicate body crumpled.

"Yikes!" Priestess exclaimed.

"H-hey!" cried High Elf Archer. At moments like this, no one moved faster than an elf. She was already in motion before Priestess could even reach out, catching the girl in arms that were far stronger than their delicate appearance would suggest.

The limp young woman's face had gone beyond pale; she was practically white now and breathing shallowly.

"This is bad news. She's got a fever," High Elf Archer reported.

"Your Highness?!" Guild Girl yelped in spite of herself. Cow Girl was likewise halfway out of her seat. You didn't have to know exactly what was going on to recognize it didn't look good. Any questions about the girl's title were swept from her head.

Cow Girl was quickly at the young woman's side; she knelt down and loosened the girl's collar. "We can't let her outfit constrict her! What else should we do?!"

"Something to drink—we have water, right?" Priestess said. "We should wipe away the sweat…"

While High Elf Archer held the girl, the others tended to her. Guild Girl watched them, stupefied, until Priestess shouted, "A doctor! My healing miracles can't do anything about sickness!"

"Understood!" Guild Girl said, snapping back to reality. She prevented herself from wasting time just nodding along.

She heard Goblin Slayer say softly, "Then I'll go, too." He leaped nimbly to his feet, unclasping his shield and the pouch at his hip in a single fluid motion to make himself lighter. "Show me where to go. And call whomever we need to call; I don't know who."

Guild Girl understood what he was asking for in his own gruff way. She used all her considerable wit to mull over the situation, then replied with much gratitude, "Yes, I will."

It's all right now. I'm calm. I can do this.

She nodded at Goblin Slayer, who nodded back. The metal helmet turned. "Apologies, but can I ask you handle things here?"

"Ask us? We're volunteerin'!" said Dwarf Shaman. Like the long-necked Lizard Priest, he was already out of his chair. Not only that: He was digging through his bag of catalysts, while Lizard Priest stood with his clawed hands and feet at the ready. It was an extraordinarily quick response to someone collapsing; they had seized the initiative, so to speak.

"Just say she's got a bit overwhelmed spectatin'."

"Indeed," Lizard Priest said. "It's all a bit too stimulating for a cultivated young lady."

They spoke pointedly, but Guild Girl agreed and indeed was grateful to them. She gave them each a quick bow.

"Don't stand on ceremony, just get goin'. This ain't lookin' good."

Dwarf Shaman waved them away, and before Guild Girl could reply "Yes, you're right," she found herself floating into the air. "Eep!"

"I'm going to run," said a voice near her abdomen. She finally registered that she had been lifted onto someone's shoulder. "Tell me where to go."

"Huh? I mean… What?!"

After that, everything happened at once. They were racing down the stadium hallway; she was being carried along at a furious pace.

They're going to think I'm *the patient like this!*

She felt confusion, panic, embarrassment, all assaulting her disheveled brain. But still, she couldn't forget the last thing she'd heard as they left. Priestess had looked at the king's little sister's neck, and in a shaking voice, she had said, "This mark…"

There are endless seeds for adventures in the Four-Cornered World. And consequently, wherever there are adventures, there will be adventurers.

§

"Things don't look good," said the handsome man, who had appeared as quickly as if he'd used a Gate spell. Yet he was the epitome of calm as he spoke.

The chamber in which King's Sister now slept was somewhat too ornate to be called a sickroom, but in any case, they had moved from there to an equally sumptuous area for receiving guests. Guild Girl looked extraordinarily tense, while Cow Girl seemed to realize only that they were in the presence of someone important.

That was understandable enough, but this was someone Priestess had met before.

In fact, between kings and queens…

…this was three or four times.

The queen of the elves, the *húsfreya* of the north, as well as the princess of the centaurs—Priestess was practically used to meeting royalty by now.

Used to it! Ha!

She had to smile for even thinking that about herself—but of course, she understood that this was no laughing matter.

"I don't believe this is any ordinary sickness," she said as she sat, her small butt practically floating on a couch softer than anything she was accustomed to. "You've seen the brand that was put upon one particular noblewoman. I suspect it's—"

"A curse," the young king concluded and nodded. "Seems likely."

Yes. Priestess nodded back but couldn't summon the word. Instead, she spared a glance at her companions. Some of them had their arms crossed and stood by the wall; some sat on the couch with her; all looked somber and thoughtful as they listened to the conversation.

The grimy man who was their leader was the most silent of all, and he simply stood there. Priestess couldn't help being amused to realize that somewhere along the line, she had been tasked with being their spokesperson.

When had that started? While she was happy to be so trusted, it also made her uneasy, even a little lonely. She found herself worrying that her rank tag, which she hoped would soon be Emerald, was just plated—a fake like her.

She realized, however, that her private insistence that she must do well was just that, *her* problem. It was self-centered.

After all, the one now under a curse was her own dear friend.

"Truth be told," the king added, "I can't claim I have no inkling as to what might be going on."

King of the land, find ye brave fighters, and then—

Just as in that silly children's song, the young king looked at the adventurers and said gravely, "When I was an adventurer myself, there was a deathless vampire who troubled the capital." Those who refused to obey such creatures could expect to face terrible tragedy.

"Where was his lair?" Goblin Slayer asked.

The king tapped his foot on the floor with a mixture of nostalgia, regret, and a coolness bordering on ruthless. "A magic cavern, an ancient place beneath the capital. He was sealed away, but the seal has been weakening."

Such had been one act of the legend about the battle in the earlier—no, now former—Dungeon of the Dead. It had happened around the same time as the All Stars, the six great heroes, were facing the Demon Lord in the abyss of the Dungeon. The young king-to-be and his party had defeated the demon, the undying king who had ruled the magical cavern, thus saving the city and earning the adventurer's place on the throne. Then he had led his forces against the Army of Darkness and repulsed it. Priestess was too young to remember it, but it was the subject of a particularly beloved saga.

"So we just have to duck back down in this cavern and fix up the seal. Problem solved, right?"

High Elf Archer's lovely voice sounded perfectly natural there in the conversation. She spoke with an ease that only fellow royalty could have, as well as the born superiority of the high elves, not to mention her natural charm. All these things came together to make it sound as if she was speaking to a friend.

Priestess noticed Guild Girl's cheek twitch, but the king paid the elf's tone no mind. He simply shook his head. "You've got the right idea, but the cavern would not be our destination. The crux of the seal is elsewhere."

"The map, sire."

Oh!

Priestess hadn't noticed the silver-haired girl attending the king until she spoke those three words. She seemed as slender as a shadow, almost fae-like. She was like High Elf Archer in that respect but different; she was as delightful as a passing breeze.

In any case, she unrolled upon the table a parchment scroll bearing a very old map.

Priestess nearly exclaimed again when she saw the place to which the young king pointed.

"There's an ancient shrine to the Earth Mother on this mountain," he explained. "Her staff is there. *It* is what holds the seal in place."

"I've heard of that," Priestess said, her voice trembling. "But I thought it was lost…"

"It was to our benefit that people should think it was."

The Earth Mother's staff was a divine instrument capable of creating a mystical barrier that repelled evil. It was supposed to have vanished, yet here the king was saying he knew where it was as casually as anything.

No…

The most important members of the Temple of the Earth Mother must have known everything. Priestess was simply too low in the hierarchy to be in on the secret.

"There is, however, a problem," the king said. "The shrine appears to be crawling with the forces of Chaos."

Was it Priestess's imagination, or did the silver-haired attendant shoot the king an urging look? If so, he didn't so much as flinch but only continued his explanation:

"The scouts we sent to investigate reported seeing goblins in the vicinity…"

"Now, that is a most unsettling detail," said Lizard Priest, raising his head like a dragon stirring from a long sleep. "The key to the capital's security fallen into the hands of Chaos?"

The king appeared to smile at this unadorned assessment. As if he was glad someone had said it. "What with the tournament on top of everything else, we've hardly been able to spare anyone."

"Seems it's true no matter where you go—hammers and flasks are always in short supply." Dwarf Shaman stroked his beard agreeably. He even took a little sip of his own most crucial possession—his wine—notwithstanding the fact that they were in the royal presence.

Guild Girl felt like she might keel over, but the king didn't seem inclined to reprimand him.

The only ones who could take wine from a dwarf were the dwarf king or that most high lady of the high elves.

"Okay, so we go get this Earth Mother's staff." High Elf Archer waved her ears to indicate that she had it all figured out and puffed out her small chest. Dwarf Shaman looked at her, clearly not convinced that she really understood. High Elf Archer took Priestess's shoulder. "This is the perfect job for you!"

"You…you think so?"

"Sure I do!"

Priestess *wasn't* sure, but High Elf Archer was trying to be encouraging.

That, however, was when the king said, "I'm afraid not," and for the first time, he sounded something less than even. He closed his eyes, took a breath, let it out, and then said briskly, "I want the girl to stay here."

Priestess took a long moment to blink: *Ummmm…*

In that time, the king's hesitation vanished. "There are several reasons. Not least that in the past, you have done well for me." The king's gaze lighted on one man, who stood by the wall as if feeling he didn't quite belong there. This man wore grimy leather armor and a cheap-looking metal helmet. "If things get out of hand, the party will be at the enemy's mercy. Hence, we can't be sending Gold-ranked into that grotto."

Why not?

"...So it's goblins?" The voice was almost mechanical, so cold it hardly seemed human.

King nodded: *That's right.* "Goblins have taken up residence in the shrine in the mountains. If we send gold-ranked adventurers, it's as good as declaring that this is no ordinary place of worship."

But...

Yes. There was another way.

"You're different. You could go to the shrine, face the goblin infestation, and—"

"W-wait just a minute! Please..." Guild Girl stood, her voice shaking. She was pale and sweating, trembling with what was obviously terror, but she spoke. "I-i-if I... If I may, sire. I'm th-the Guild staff member responsible for him." Her voice went up an octave, then cracked. She sucked in a few painful-sounding breaths. "As such... *Ahem.* Well, a request like that... I'm afraid..."

I can't countenance it was what she wanted to say, but the words simply wouldn't come out.

How else was she supposed to feel? He was now, beyond question and with all esteem, a Silver-ranked adventurer. He had spent years reaching that point, and she had spent years watching him. Finally, he was here. The world was ahead of him.

And he was still going to be pigeonholed as a goblin hunter? Would he be sent to slay goblins all his life?

I don't want to...to give him back.

Wasn't he an accomplished, perfectly respectable Silver-ranked adventurer?

But...

But that was exactly why there was no other answer to this problem, and Guild Girl knew it.

Who else was there to go? Who else besides the five—no, four—Silver-ranked adventurers here?

Well and good. But this request came from the king himself. And *he* was going to have to refuse it? True, it wouldn't be listed in the official records—but that was exactly why it could leave a black mark.

And besides, when it came to slaying goblins, who else was there? Who else could—?

"I don't mind," came a low voice.

"Wha...?"

"I said, I don't mind."

A short, brusque whisper. A muffled sound from beneath the helmet. *Why?*

Guild Girl didn't voice the question, yet the helmet turned to her. He looked at her from behind his visor and nodded. "Because," he said, then paused briefly before he resumed. "I once received help."

For a second, Guild Girl wasn't sure what he was talking about—but then she realized it was the time, years ago, when he had been faced with a horde of goblins. At that moment, when he had been powerless to do anything, she was the one who had turned everything around.

She hadn't done it with any idea of earning gratitude or putting him in her debt. "N-no, I wasn't trying to...," she said, but the rest wouldn't quite come out.

He shifted from his spot, then moved between her and the king as if to protect her. "If there are goblins, then I'll go."

"...So you're accepting?" the king asked.

"Yes."

Finally, he felt as if all the gears had clicked together.

When I come right down to it, I'm an outsider here.

He could visit the capital, observe the festivities, take in the tournament, and yes, it was exciting. But it was not where he belonged. Until a situation like this arose, he had no part to play.

And having no part to play was a wonderful thing indeed.

But I don't mind.

He decided that this was well and good and stepped forward.

He would deal with the goblins in front of him and then go on to the next thing. That was enough.

That was enough—it was enough to reward him.

"I don't quite understand, but...," his childhood friend began, her voice reaching his ears in the stillness. No, she wouldn't know exactly what was going on. Even he didn't, really.

Politics, matters of state, the kingship. He understood none of it.

He understood only that he was needed. And thus, there was only one thing to do.

"But...you're going on an adventure. Right?" she said.

"No," he said with a slow shake of his head. This was no adventure. "I am going to slay goblins."

That was why they called him Goblin Slayer.

"Th-thank you very much!" the young girl with black hair said as she hopped off the wagon. The pack on her back jostled as she bowed to her benefactor.

"Don't mention it. I was grateful to have someone to travel with me," replied a young woman, also with black hair. Hers was tied in a single braid, held in place with a rose ornament. At her hip was a katana. She looked to be about the same age as the first girl, but her bare feet suggested she was a rhea. "I've got four people in my party, but everyone is multi-classed as a warrior and a wizard…"

It was a relief to have a specialist on the front row.

"Heh-heh," the first girl said to that, blushing.

"You're here to see the tournament as well, yes?"

"Oh, uh, *ahem*," said the girl with the name like a storm, like a primordial whirlwind, nodding eagerly. "And, um, the capital, too…" She wanted to do some sightseeing, she added awkwardly, her voice threatening to trail off into silence.

The rhea fencer woman, so far from making fun of her, accepted this with a simple "I see." Then she said, "As a matter of fact, we're new to the capital as well."

"You are?"

"Yes. Should we see each other again, I hope it will be a favorable meeting."

The girl nodded earnestly, her head bobbing up and down.

"Farewell, then," the rhea woman said and started walking away. The black-haired girl watched them go —the party also included a female cleric so lovely the girl was almost smitten with her, an elderly lizardman, and a hale young elf.

She watched until they vanished into the crowds, then let out a breath.

I'm finally on my own, she thought. There she was, standing smack amid the fearsome (!) crowds of the capital. She had no clear objective to speak of. She'd simply heard that there was going to be a tournament and had decided she'd like to see it.

She had realized with a start that if she chose to come here or not, no one would criticize her. Back in her village, every friend and neighbor would have had an opinion, but she wasn't there anymore. She was an adventurer. She was on her own. She was free.

She'd quickly checked what was in her purse, asked the Guild employee about how much it would cost to travel, and factored in that she would want some spending money. She'd been taking adventures here and there, quests she thought she could do, and saving up a bit of money—and it led her to this moment.

"......I really made it."

She could hardly believe it herself. Here she was now in a place she had never imagined she would be, never thought she'd see with her own eyes.

The sight that spread out before her was something she had never even dreamed of.

The girl started to bounce up and down, testing the ground under her feet.

It's the feeling of the capital's ground!

She looked up, and although her vision should have been blocked by the tall buildings, she somehow felt she could see the sky, low overhead. The sounds she heard, the smells that drifted to her, the crowds of people—none of it was familiar.

I think my head's gonna start spinning...

She gripped her bouncing onyx charm firmly to help slow her speeding heart. Taking a job as a guard for the wagon had allowed her to get here and save a lot on travel.

Now what do I do?

What should she spend her money on? Food? Snacks? Clothes? Accessories? Maybe weapons or armor? Oh, and would they want an admission fee to see the tournament? Surely they would, right? What was she going to do…?

"Uh, umm…"

Bewildered, the girl took a step toward the side of the street, watching the path closely and thinking. She believed it was important to stop and think sometimes, and she was very good at it.

She'd come to the capital. She was going to see the tournament. She wanted to have some fun. And also do it on her own. In that case…

I need to find somewhere to stay.

She would rent a room at an inn, somewhere in the capital, and stay there—all by herself!

It would be the first time she had done such a thing. She'd never even heard someone else talk about doing it.

If she was going to make the effort, then she'd like to stay somewhere big. Hmm. Somewhere big…

"I know!"

Suddenly and somewhat belatedly restless, the girl jogged toward the edge of the great thoroughfare.

I'll go see the castle!

This was, after all, the capital. The place where the king was. If you hadn't seen the castle, had you even really been there?

The girl worked her way toward her new destination, buffeted this way and that by the crowds. Thankfully, the castle was the most conspicuous building in the city. She wouldn't get lost. She was small enough that the crowds threatened to bury her, but if she stood on her tiptoes, she could see the place.

She soon made her way there. The castle stood beside a competition ground (apparently this was different from the coliseum proper!). In the girl's eyes, it looked like a massive mansion, a baffling collection of pillars and hallways.

She wasn't so far off about that. The royal family that now ruled this city had simply renovated the palace they inherited, which was far older than the founding of this nation.

In fact, all the capital's appointments, starting with the aqueducts, were like that. The palace with all its majesty was the same—and the girl was sure she had never seen such a large building in her entire life.

"You're really gonna be part of it?"

"Not if it's only sword fighting—I'd be hopeless. But if there's horse riding, that's a different story!"

"You can't stop her. She'll never listen to you!"

The young girl wasn't the only one taking in the castle; crowds of people pressed toward the place. The girl was looking up from the seething, churning crowd when her eyes met those of one other particular person.

It was yet another young woman with black hair; she wore green robes emblazoned with the symbol of the Trade God and carried an iron spear. She was chatting with two party members who stood with her, but when she saw the girl, she flashed a toothy grin, smiled like the sun, and shot her a thumbs-up.

"...!"

She started to come over. Our young traveler was taken by surprise; she didn't know what any of this was about. She just thought the girl looked cool. She looked at the other young woman, her eyes shining, which seemed to please the object of her interest. The girl in green laughed aloud, when—

"My goodness!" someone exclaimed.

A figure had appeared on the southern balcony, which allowed one to observe competitions without leaving the castle. The girl hopped up and down, trying to get a look at their face, but she couldn't quite see. She could, though, hear the voices of the three adventurers:

"Hey, who's that?"

"Isn't that the princess?"

"You think?"

The princess! Now she definitely wanted to see. The girl stretched and strained, pushing among the wall of people.

"I don't know. I don't think it *feels* like her."

"Maybe she's just too far away to tell."

"You think...???"

Hoo...hah! The girl finally broke through the mass of bodies and got a view of the balcony. There, indeed, stood the princess, resplendent with her golden hair and white dress.

And yet...

Why does she look so...uncomfortable?

CHAPTER 3

COOL RUNNING

There was a staff there. A divine instrument sent to this land long, long ago, when the gods had occupied themselves with war games. Any who took it in hand could wield it as a "hero unit," protecting Order against evil.

But all that was now far in the past.

Long had the staff slept that bore the Earth Mother's name. Ten years ago and more, it had been wielded to drive back the evil and death encroaching upon the capital, but even that had been only for an instant.

The Earth Mother's staff had been sealed away in the deepest reaches of an ancient shrine—ancient ruins—to safeguard the Four-Cornered World.

This burgeoning power was enough to destroy anybody. The fate of the world of people was not decided by the gods: This was one of the golden rules the gods had set upon watching over the Four-Cornered World.

And so the Earth Mother's staff went to sleep.

Nothing, however, impinged upon its holiness, not even when the forces of Chaos came to establish themselves in the shrine.

"GOROGB…"

"GOBB! GRBB."

Nothing so lowly as a goblin would even be allowed to touch the staff. Goblins, however, did not wonder *why* they couldn't touch the staff but only grew angry about it.

Which was, in its own way, a stroke of good fortune. If they could have touched it, the ensuing calamity would have been terrible indeed.

"GBBR?"

So what happened was no doubt because a goblin, flush with impatience, had jumped onto the altar.

It started with a pebble.

The goblin would never have spotted it clicking as it fell from the wall. Goblins, on the whole, are not blind—but they pay very little attention to what they see. A goblin, with his minimal passive perception, would have struggled to notice such a thing at all.

Although perhaps he would have noticed the wall shivering after the pebble fell...

"GRGB?!"

So what if he did? What could something as lowly as a goblin do about it?

The first one died when the wall came crashing outward. Even the other goblins noticed this, and for a second, they hesitated between guffawing at their idiotic comrade and running away.

"Four goblins! I mean, three! Weapons, uh... Argh! Look for yourself!!"

"GOROGBB?!?!!!?"

The delay was critical.

No sooner had the words been spoken than one goblin found an arrow going clean through the roof of his mouth and out the back of his head.

The other goblins were enraged, though they didn't spare a glance at the tumbling corpse.

An elf!

An elf woman!

Let's drag her down and make her weep!!

Their brains filled with the sweet fragrance of that feminine flesh—a most convenient distraction. The goblins charged forward. What was one female? They could beat her into submission with their clubs. Even if it cost a few of their lives.

"GROG! GOOROGB!!"

"GOBBGR!!"

This was why goblins never rose to be any more than what they were.

"That's one...!"

"GOOB?!"

A scruffy-looking man emerged from behind the elf and flung the sword he held in his right hand. His aim was true, piercing the throat of one goblin; the creature fell back, clawing at his neck.

Goblin Slayer jumped forward, kicking the corpse out of the way and pulling his sword out of it almost in a single movement.

Two left. No problems. One of them came at him from the side; he rebuffed the creature with his shield.

"GROGB?!"

"Hrm...!" Without hesitating a moment, he rolled forward. Another goblin had used his companion's attack as a distraction, a chance to leap at Goblin Slayer.

A rusty sword scraped along the stone, and the two goblins tumbled headlong into each other.

Goblin Slayer was not going to give them time to start squabbling about it. This was a decisive opportunity.

"Eeeeyyaaahhhh!"

With a screech, a massive figure slammed its tail into one of the goblins' heads, meanwhile smashing the other's spine with the heel of its foot. When you come right down to it, there's no better weapon than sufficient mass combined with sufficient speed.

The battle didn't even last a full turn. All the goblins that had taken up residence in the chamber were annihilated.

The adventurers landed with puffs of dust. They were followed by a small figure scrambling out of the wall. "Gods! Tunnel won't break through the wall, I says! So combine it with Weathering, he says! Who *does* that?!"

"I thought it would be the fastest way." Goblin Slayer's reply to the griping dwarf was concise.

Dwarf Shaman replied that Ruta would be very happy—which wasn't quite a compliment and wasn't quite a complaint.

It had been very much the sort of solution one might have expected from a follower of the god who always sought a faster, better result. It would also have been impossible if they hadn't already known about the layout of these particular ruins. There is, after all, a reason that most adventurers in most places start at the *entrance* to a dungeon.

"And?" asked Lizard Priest, who was busy finishing off the goblin he had stepped on. "Where is the famous staff?"

"I doubt the goblins have taken it. It must be nearby." Goblin Slayer's helmet turned this way and that until his gaze found the altar.

There upon it was a staff carved with the image of a familiar winged woman. At first glance, it could almost have appeared to be a dilapidated stick of metal—except it was anything but. To still exist after all these countless ages proved that it was no ordinary staff. One did not have to know about its magical properties or miraculous capabilities to see that much; one needed only to observe the materials.

Time had not conquered the metal nor cracked its surface. This must be adamantite.

"There it is," was all Goblin Slayer said and immediately reached for it.

"Hold it," someone said, pressing back his filthy gauntlet. A delicate arm reached out and took the staff. It was High Elf Archer. "If you touched this thing with *those* hands, I'll bet the Earth Mother wouldn't have been happy!"

"I see." Goblin Slayer grunted.

Lizard Priest's eyes rolled merrily in his head. "I daresay none of us are worthy of this instrument."

"Because this is a weapon that can only be used by the Earth Mother's believers, ain't it?" Dwarf Shaman was tossing some candies to the swiftly closing hole to show his gratitude.

It was hardly unusual for adventurers to be left tearing their hair out when they discovered at the end of a lengthy quest that the magic item they'd obtained was, say, an ax that only dwarves could use.

"Doesn't really matter. We're not actually going to use it," High Elf Archer said. It wasn't a weapon anyway. As far as she was concerned, those were the salient points.

Her delicate fingers wrapped around the staff, and she lifted it from the altar in a single quick motion.

There was a tense instant—but nothing happened.

"I really wish we could have brought the kid along," High Elf Archer said, her flat chest rising and falling with her breathing. She was trying to lighten the mood. She placed the staff across her shoulder. "Don't you think she would have been better off with us?"

"If she were here, I doubt we could have completed the king's quest," said Goblin Slayer, who was still looking in every direction, never letting his guard falter. He didn't sense goblins. Had anyone or anything noticed the fight just now? He wasn't sure. But he knew they should hurry. He was still running calculations in a corner of his mind as he spoke, deliberately forcing himself to keep a flat, restrained tone. "Breaking and entering I can do, but I'm not suited to urban adventuring."

"I'm not saying *you* should be the one to do it."

"Maybe so, but y'know who else ain't suited to it? An anvil!" Dwarf Shaman snickered, rejoining the conversation. "It'd never work—you just scream *princess*!"

"Come over here and say that to my face!" High Elf Archer snapped, and they were off and running. Just another of the arguments that had perdured between high elves and dwarves since the Age of the Gods.

However, the girl who would normally have watched them with a concerned—but accustomed—expression was nowhere to be seen. Could it be that the pair's boisterous exchanges were in part a way of supporting her very existence?

Lizard Priest was not so barbaric as to point this out. He slithered his long neck, his tongue slipping out from between his jaws with all his love for battle, and said to their leader, "Well then, milord Goblin Slayer. Shall we do just as we planned?"

"Yes," Goblin Slayer replied. "We press forward and hit them from behind."

"The little devils never do think *they'll* be the ones to get ambushed!"

"It would defeat the point if any of them were able to use our hole to get outside. We should finish this in one fell swoop." Goblin Slayer was brief, decisive. A completely different person from when he was taking in the tournament in the capital.

High Elf Archer, still engaged in her argument, flicked her ears. *He's feeling lively.* But that was certainly nothing to be pleased about. She sighed an extremely elegant sigh.

The metal helmet asked, "What's the matter?"

"Nothing much," she said, her ears wiggling. "It's just, I guess I shouldn't be surprised how the student turned out with a teacher like this."

"Don't be ridiculous."

She didn't love that answer. Her beautiful eyebrows arched in annoyance, and she spun on her heel—though she looked like a dancer doing it. The next second, a delicate white finger was poking Goblin Slayer in the helmet. "What? Going to claim you're not her teacher?"

"I grant I instructed her to some extent. However..." *However.* A mutter: "What she has accomplished is all the fruit of her own labor."

High Elf Archer seemed to like this better. "Huh!" she intoned, her eyebrows taking on a curve of pleasure this time. "Good enough. If she's going to buy us some time, then we better get on with the adventuring..."

That was when they heard it: a *plik, plik, plik* of scraping rock echoing around the room.

Being adventurers, they all reacted instantaneously, drawing their weapons, dropping into fighting stances, preparing themselves for whatever came next.

And then they saw it.

They had taken it to be one of the statues decorating the chamber. It towered up to the very ceiling, and now it moved.

"———MA...!!!!" it roared and raised its brutal arms.

"Turns out the gods don't like it when you try to steal their toys!" Dwarf Shaman chirped.

"Don't try to blame this on me!" High Elf Archer shouted back. "If anyone here is in for some divine punishment, it's Orcbolg!"

"So it's some sort of moving statue..." Goblin Slayer had no idea that it was a monster called a golem. He did know, however, that he was in the company of someone who knew more about stone than anyone. "What do you think?" he asked.

"Swords won't be helpin' us against *that*," Dwarf Shaman replied.

The statue rumbled, its joints shaking and screeching as it began to move forward. It reached out, worked its legs, and slammed its fist down.

It was like a hammer blow against the floor of the chamber, but the adventurers leaped back and managed to avoid it. Pebbles and bits of rock came raining down. Dwarf Shaman growled, "If we had a hammer or a maul, we could finish this in one shot!"

"Smashing weapons?" Goblin Slayer looked at the bits of goblin that came tumbling toward his feet, then grunted. "Hmm."

Then he grabbed the staff out of High Elf Archer's hands and, without another thought, flung it through the air.

The Earth Mother's sacred instrument was grabbed in its flight by a huge, scaled hand that held it fast.

"Then smash!" Goblin Slayer said.

"So I shall!"

There followed a blow no less stupendous than the one the monster had struck. The huge statue took the attack on the hip, reeling backward and slamming into the wall.

"Hah!" cried Lizard Priest, the breath hot in his nostrils. To stand on two legs without even a tail to lean on was sheer foolishness! "Still, I would prefer not to use this weapon!"

"I told you, it's not a weapon!" High Elf Archer shouted, completely ignoring the golem, which was struggling to stand back up. Arrows wouldn't work on it anyway, she decided. Instead, she was watching the passageway that extended out of the chamber. With all this roaring and crashing, the goblins might notice them…

Then again, they're such cowards, she thought. They wouldn't dare come into the room.

"What will you do if it breaks?!" she called.

"If this was all it took to break it, *they* would have done it a long time ago," Goblin Slayer said.

"Fair enough…," she replied, but privately she vowed to give him a good kick later—seeing as, despite her glance at the ceiling, no heavenly punishment from the Earth Mother appeared to be forthcoming for him.

The goddess seemed to be hiding her face more and more recently.

©Noboru Kannatuki

"Oh well… I guess an adamantium staff's perfect for this sort of work," Dwarf Shaman mumbled, not interested in arguing. Instead, he focused on watching Lizard Priest bring the staff to bear.

To reiterate: There's no better weapon than sufficient mass combined with sufficient speed. The effort involved in reducing the golem to rubble was nothing compared to the effort Priestess was expending at that exact moment.

Which is to say, it was a very easy thing indeed.

§

This was *not* easy.

"I knew this would happen…!" the rhea girl grumbled—but she was careful to do so in a corner of the competition field, where no one could hear her. She removed her helmet and peeled off her balaclava; she took a deep breath, which brought with it the sweet musk of her own sweat.

Wizard Boy, however, paid no attention—this was hardly the time. He was too busy grabbing a kerchief and tossing it to the girl in the saddle. He was also grumbling angrily, but his gaze was forward.

"They can't *be* knocked off their horses," he growled.

On the far side of the coliseum, which heaved with the passion of the audience, was a knight replacing a shattered lance—a centaur knight.

Actually, Wizard Boy wasn't even sure it was appropriate to call him a knight. Not out of discrimination but as a matter of definition: It was impossible for a centaur to mount up. Which gave them a definitive advantage in mounted jousting…

"But you didn't fall off, either, and that's what counts. The score's even."

I'd like to meet the buffoon who thought centaurs and humans should face each other in combat.

Since the opponent couldn't be unhorsed, an ordinary knight was at a decisive disadvantage. The fact that his partner was holding on at all with her tiny stature was testament to her force of will, but that didn't matter to the score.

The centaur at least had the good grace to look guilty, but it wasn't going to make him hold back—no warrior worth their salt would.

That was fine. He felt no anger about someone trying to achieve victory under the rules as stipulated. Instead, his frustration and the rhea girl's were directed at whomever had deemed this situation acceptable.

Never mind that, if you trawled the history books, there were war songs that described a young lion crossing spears with a centaur.

"What *really* hacks me off—," the girl started—they were in an interval, a resting time, between bouts. She wiped off the sweat, wetted her parched throat, and took a bite of dried meat, her umpteenth lunch of the day. "—is that if I win this, that paladin gets to go around grinning like he was right all along!"

The boy could readily imagine it, but he tried to keep a calm front as he grinned. "Let me guess—you still don't plan on losing."

"I damn well don't!"

"Perfect." He was glad to hear it. If she'd sounded like she was giving up before the battle even began, he'd planned to advise her to expend the minimum of stamina and go for victory in the swordsmanship contest. But if she was ready... "Then we're here to win. Think you can do it?"

"I assume you have a plan?" She glanced at him, and her smile was like the sun. "Better believe I'm going to do it!"

He actually had to avert his eyes from her earnest gaze, coughing discreetly. Then he closed his eyes for a second, took a deep breath, and said as casually as he could, "You're already down low, so take advantage of that to strike with your lance from a low position. That's the key."

"Right."

"It also means your opponent is going to have to aim low, down over the tilt."

"Right," the girl said again and nodded.

"Okay," the boy said. He waited a beat, and then he told her the plan.

"......You really think that's gonna work?" the girl asked. It sounded a little underhanded to her.

He responded to her unease with a confident "No problem. A song from the east says that if you want to strike down a man, first you have to strike down his horse."

And because the centaurs came from the plains to the east, the opponent would no doubt be familiar with the saying.

"That makes sense!" Rhea Fighter said. Her eyes shone, but really, Wizard Boy was just saying what he had to. If you didn't go into a contest with confidence, then you could lose even when you should have won.

She said she could win, and she intended to. Anyone trying to put frivolous distractions in her mind could go get kicked by a horse.

"...He's not a horse anyway," Wizard Boy added.

"Oh, good point," the rhea girl said, clapping her hands innocently. "So it's from underneath, like this." She made some sort of gesture, her armor clanking as she moved. Wizard Boy didn't know much about martial arts, and he didn't fully understand what she was implying. But then she said, "One good thrust, right?"

"Yeah!" He nodded. "We aren't looking to hurt anyone."

"Sure, that's true."

"Then there's the shout. Bellow as loud as you can—make sure it comes from deep in your belly."

"Right...!"

The girl nodded, and then the boy handed her the balaclava and helped her slide her helmet over it. He gave her a gentle tap on the head just before she lowered her visor, helped her up onto her donkey, and sent her on her way. Now there was nothing he could do but watch.

If this is an adventure...

Rhea Fighter rode off on her donkey, a fresh lance in her hand. As he watched her go, Wizard Boy gave a quick shake of his head and said, "No..."

No.

Is *this an adventure?*

Wizard Boy couldn't understand how that pigheaded old rhea thought, but his view of the world probably deserved Wizard Boy's attention. He had asked them: Was it ruthless, sending a single rhea to retrieve a gemstone from a dragon's den? He who can't send his friends off and trust them as they go is either very arrogant or doesn't really think of them as friends at all.

If they'd believed for a second that rhea would pocket the stone for himself, they would all have gone charging in together instead—and would certainly have been wiped out.

I'll never make such a stupid mistake.

So it was that the boy clenched his fist and simply watched the rhea girl ride forth to challenge the centaur. The tiny figure mounted on a donkey looked as brave as she did comical.

Even if the girl won this round, it might be a fluke. There might not be a next time. She was facing a horse person, after all; she had as much chance as that mournful old man against his windmills.

But who gives a shit?!

The rhea girl snorted under her helmet. Who would dare to laugh at that chivalry-mad old man? Hadn't he believed that chivalry *was* possible, to the bitter end? That was why he had challenged the four-armed giant. The Four-Cornered World might be wide, but how many people could there be in it who would challenge a giant all on their own?

She hadn't known the story until she heard it from her master, and he had said, *"Some might think the old man merely a fool, but what story of a mere fool ever lasted so long?"*

I want to be like him.

That was the thought in her mind as she put the spurs to her donkey. "Yaaaaahhhh!"

Her mount accelerated, rushing forward, the force of it throwing her back in her saddle. The centaur knight raced to meet her. She heard hoofbeats, like the roar of a waterfall—not that she had ever seen one.

The rhea girl couched her lance firmly, ignoring the cloud of dust. The contest would be decided in one instant. She opened her eyes as wide as she could, trying to see past her own visor.

So fast. They were both moving so quickly. She didn't have any precise numbers, but she could see the distance closing. It would be one second more.

"Listen," the boy had said. The opponent had the edge on her in speed, mass, and physical force. Even the girl's position was disadvantageous; coming up from below was not as powerful as coming down from above.

In which case…

You don't have to thrust yourself into that situation!

"Rrraahhh!"

The lance came crashing down from over her head. There was an earsplitting shout. She refused to lose. She clenched her abdominal muscles.

"Keeeeeeeehhhh!"

With an animalistic yell, the rhea girl strained her entire body. The centaur's eyes were wide. He even smiled at her.

Up coming down, down coming up. The lance points slid past each other. A draw, then? No, it wasn't.

The centaur's lance grazed the rhea girl's shield and was deflected to the side. That was the opening she needed; her lance was through.

The centaur practically threw himself against her weapon. Its trajectory was like a wildfire reaching upward—except it was almost completely horizontal.

She rammed the lance home, striking the centaur's shield from the left as hard as she could. Unlike with a human knight, there was no horse's head there. Which meant... Which meant...

He's got to be leaning forward!

Wood splintered, the impact running like lightning through the girl's small hands, making everything numb.

But so what?!

The rhea girl braced herself in her stirrups; her small body was forced backward, but she stayed in the saddle. Behind her, there was a thump as the centaur tumbled sidelong into the dirt.

Chatter broke out in the audience. The rhea girl brought her donkey around and took in the scene dumbly, not sure whether she had actually won.

The centaur's servant was quickly at his side. The centaur wouldn't be dead. The judges looked at one another.

That's right: Just because someone couldn't be unhorsed didn't mean they couldn't be knocked down. Tumbles were usually adjudged to be the fault of the mount and therefore not a defeat—but when horse and rider were one, then surely it was the knight who was responsible.

If her opponent wasn't in violation of the rules, then surely neither was she. And as such...

"Knock 'im the hell over." That was the plan the boy had given her. The boy who was now sprinting toward her from the other end of the field.

Defend, then strike—and when they were at a draw, she would make her move.

She'd been raised to seize the initiative at every moment, and it seemed like madness to her. But...if the limping old rhea—the one who had taught her how to use a stick—could see it, what would he say? Would he get that fond look in his eye and tell her, *Not bad...for the likes of you?*

Nah... Probably not.

Her grandpa, just like her current instructor, wasn't much for praise. Although he wasn't much for humiliation, either.

"You did it...!"

So it was that the boy, rushing up with his face red as an apple, was the only one. The only one who had words of unvarnished approbation for her—even if he didn't say *everything* he felt.

"I did...I did it!" The girl tore off her helmet, jumped off her donkey, and leaped toward him.

Speed and mass. Unable to hold her up, the boy exclaimed, and they ended up in a tangle on the ground.

On the other side of the field, the judges were raising a large flag in the rhea girl's direction.

§

"Th...that was excellent..."

In the spectator seats, Priestess applauded awkwardly, somehow managing to maintain something that could pass for a smile.

Everything felt so constrained, so discomfiting. Nothing felt quite right; it was like someone had a hold of both her shoulders. The makeup made her face itch, while the way her hair was pulled back tugged at her cheeks and forehead and made her whole visage tense.

And this dress! It pinched her chest, which had been rather shoved into the outfit, while her hips had nearly given up the ghost, the fit was so tight. She could hardly believe princesses endured such garments every day.

"What's the matter? *Ahem*—I mean, is anything distressing you, Your Majesty?"

"If there's anything you need, please don't hesitate to tell us."

"Su-sure…"

I'm not sure this is quite fair…

Such must have been the thought in the minds of the two ladies-in-waiting who stood behind her, one with red hair and one with gold. Guild Girl, who was the daughter of nobility, Priestess could understand, but how could the girl from the farm seem so at ease? Priestess was uncomprehending—but she couldn't let it show on her face. Instead, she sat there stiff as a doll.

"Indeed! Absolutely indeed!"

The biggest issue of all was the person who sat applauding beside her—the man who called himself a paladin of the Supreme God. "This is the epitome of equality! Is it not wonderful?"

"Er, uh, well…"

He took note of her every move, her every shift; she felt like she was under constant surveillance.

He claimed to be a representative there on behalf of the Temple of the Supreme God, and he seemed to be acquainted with the king's little sister. Just trying to make sure she didn't slip up in some matter of etiquette was exhausting.

At the same time, she couldn't help noticing…

He's nothing like the Lady Archbishop.

In fact, he wasn't like any of the other followers of the Supreme God that Priestess knew. Not the cleric with whom she'd become friends in the frontier town nor the inspector at the Guild. His proud self-possession reminded her of that female knight, but…no, it wasn't quite the same.

How could she put it…?

It was the difference between someone *trying* to be righteous and someone who assumed they already were.

"I thought she was at quite a disadvantage…," Priestess ventured.

"By no means!" Consider the way the paladin responded to Priestess's doubts with full confidence, as if he himself had achieved the feat. "They each made the fullest use of the abilities they were born with! A follower of the Earth Mother must be more enlightened."

©Noboru Kannatuki

He sounded like he would put a fish on dry land and encourage it to run. Priestess still had questions, but she chose not to voice them. She suspected the paladin would happily continue to talk anyway.

"Sometimes, Your Highness… Your Highness?"

"Er…oh!" Priestess blinked. "Yes?"

"Sometimes I see the great festivals and think, *We must reform the Earth Mother's ceremonies.*"

"Um… How so?"

"I'm referring to the dancing girl at the harvest festival." Priestess cocked her head, so the paladin of the Supreme God continued. "Her outfit shows far too much skin for a young woman! No cleric should appear like that in public."

"Ah…" Priestess sounded a bit strained, but she managed a facial expression whose exact meaning was open to interpretation.

After all, she was herself one of those who had appeared in this outfit that one must never wear in public. Now, years after the fact, she was able to see it for the honor it had been. Not that she felt or had felt no embarrassment—but the pride was greater.

I was so inexperienced back then…

Of course, she still had much growing to do even now.

That was an excellent adventure.

The paladin of the Supreme God continued to argue, even as Priestess let her thoughts wander. From questioning the propriety of such garments in public, the logic quickly took a leap. The ritual cast doubt on the moral character of the dancers. It inflamed the desires of the spectating believers. Which was to say, it could be taken to suggest that the Earth Mother herself was a seductress. By extension, it was an offense to all women!

He didn't even spare the maidens who trod on the grapes of the early harvest. How could they say that showing skin was immoral yet work the grapes in their bare feet?

"I can't believe that any woman would engage in such activities willingly. Reform is necessary at the earliest possible…"

Priestess was only half listening, but she thought she could hear the blood rushing to her head. His words reminded her of long-ago events that had been an embarrassment to people she treasured. A foolish plot that they had at last undone, and now he wanted to drag the entire thing through the mud again.

Anger boiled in the pit of her stomach, but she forced it down.

No... Don't do it...

She focused everything she had on breathing in, then forced herself to breathe out as calmly as possible. She had to resist letting her emotions make her cause a scene—or go drinking, as she had before.

And yet... She glanced at the two women behind her, who both wore awkward smiles. *I guess it's not my place to speak on the princess's behalf.*

Priestess privately pouted, wishing the others would think about what *she* was going through. That's right: She actually pouted.

They didn't all have to go away and leave me...

Of course, she understood the situation. She knew it was what it was. She understood she had been given this role because she was the only one who could do it—so she would do it as best she could.

Even so, she wasn't thrilled at being left behind, dissatisfaction born of her burgeoning awareness of herself as a halfway decent adventurer. (Although she hadn't yet noticed that she herself had cultivated that precious treasure.)

"Is that so? I see," she said. After the rush of anger and frustration, she constrained herself to a nod and a few words. A pleasant smile. "Thank you for telling me how you see things."

"...Is that all you have to say?"

Priestess gave the paladin a questioning look. "Yes? I believe it is..."

He leaned toward her eagerly, seeming to have forgotten where he was and who he was ostensibly with. "Does that mean, then, that you have no intention of correcting these injustices within the Temple of the Earth Mother?!"

"Why would I?"

"Why?! Have I not pointed out the problems to you?!"

"Yes, and I heard you."

"Then why do you not seek to do something about them?!"

"Because you and I are different people."

The paladin of the Supreme God was stunned into silence. His already pale, noble face grew even whiter, drained of blood. Priestess had a passing thought: that he looked almost like ash. Like the white ash that remains after everything else has burned away.

"Well, then…," he managed to squeeze out, his voice like settling ashes. "Do you believe that this disordered, this chaotic Four-Cornered World should simply remain as it is?"

"Umm…," Priestess said, tapping her pointer finger against her lip in thought. "I'm not really sure."

There! The man's lips curled in an ugly expression of triumph. His smile ridiculed everything about her: her shallow thoughts, her ignorance, her narrowness of vision.

"I mean, I'm friends with an elf, a lizardman, a dwarf…even a centaur," Priestess said, smiling right back at him, paying no heed at all to his expression.

There were adventurers, and there were also princesses. There were nobles, and there were merchants. Farmers. Waitresses at taverns. Priestess had never once thought of them as disordered or disorganized or one better than the other.

"The desert to the east is hot, and the north is cold. The plains are wide, but the forest is dense."

She remembered the Innsmouth, the fish-people she'd met when they slew a sea serpent—it seemed like it would be very hard for them to live on land. And yet in the tavern Goblin Slayer had taken her to, there had been a fish-people barmaid. A lovely girl in perfect clothes, making beer—Priestess thought her very cool.

Then again, maybe everyone wore adorable outfits while making alcohol—she thought of her senior cleric stomping on the grapes.

The people she met might have been of all kinds, yet all of them were joyful from deep within. How many chances did you get to play around in bare feet, after all?

In the desert, on the other hand, it was boiling (not just hot!), too punishing to show much skin, and that had been a challenge. And yet as overdressed as she'd felt at the time, if she'd gone to the icy seas of the north in that outfit, she would have been frozen stiff.

Now that I think about it, I've really gone to a lot of places and met a lot of people.

The thought drifted pleasantly through her mind, and she shook her head gently from side to side. "Trying to fit all those people into just one thing... It's not— Uhhh, I mean... Hmm."

Indeed, it seemed impossible. But that didn't mean that, within her, some were worthier than others. When she realized that, Priestess finally felt the pieces fall into place.

"I think maybe everyone *likes* being different, and it's important for us to accept that," she said.

Yes. Priestess nodded as if to affirm her own words. She was sure. She knew there were people who disliked things that she loved, while there were probably people who loved things that she found intolerable. The *húsfreya* of the north was trying to learn a new language, and the centaur racers set crowds of every kind cheering.

And yet Priestess had found the culture of the north dizzying, and the centaur princess had claimed adventurers made no sense to her. To be different was not to say you couldn't walk together, and to walk together is not to say everything had to be the same.

"Anyway, that's what I think," Priestess concluded, and then she scratched her cheek, a bit embarrassed, a bit shy. She'd only said what was on her mind, and although she'd said it quite fluently, it would never have passed as a proper sermon.

More to the point, she wondered if maybe the "king's little sister" shouldn't have spoken so freely...

"...You sound like one of those people who want to claim that even goblins have their virtues," the paladin said.

That made Priestess freeze. She turned to look at him, and he snorted in disgust.

He hasn't...figured me out, has he? She glanced at the two women behind her, but they were both shaking their heads.

Of course not. He didn't know. Priestess put her hand to her chest, now slightly larger because of the padding, and breathed a sigh of relief.

Still...

That subject came up awfully suddenly.

"They exist, you know," Priestess said. "Good goblins."

"...What?" the man asked, incredulous.

Priestess smiled. "Didn't you know? The sea goblins—they were wonderful people." The paladin looked positively flummoxed. Priestess then added, "I grant, the gillmen don't much like being called that."

But it was okay.

This was the question she'd been asking herself since the day she became an adventurer.

She looked the paladin straight in the eye. "Yes... I daresay there might be a good goblin out there."

He goggled at her. This was obviously completely unexpected to him. Although she wasn't sure if he was more baffled by the fact that she didn't agree with him or by the answer she had given.

"True, a 'good goblin' would be one that didn't attack humans. He would probably still hate people and probably still think stealing was good. I don't think that would change."

The Four-Cornered World was wider, bigger, more complex and varied than anyone knew. There were good things and also bad things. And while one couldn't simply accept the bad things, still... Yes, even still...

"The world will never be quite the way I want it or quite the way you want it."

There were certain things that should be done. Things that even the gods had entrusted to Fate and Chance.

"..."

For a moment, the man didn't say anything—although Priestess thought she caught the sound of grinding teeth. Then he exclaimed, "You must pardon me! It seems you fail to understand what our *true* problems are!"

You can practically smell the ash on him.

That was the aroma Priestess detected as the man stood up from his chair so fast he almost kicked it over and exited the room at a brisk stride—different from that *other* person's.

Priestess didn't bother to watch him go but slumped against the back of her chair, letting it hold her up.

"...Considering he was watching the proceedings in a noble box with the king's own little sister, his manners seemed somewhat lacking." Priestess heard a sigh from behind; it was Guild Girl, half scowling and half chuckling.

Still slumped in the chair in a most unladylike fashion, Priestess gave the woman behind her a dubious look. "Did I go too far...?"

"It was a theological debate. I would say you went just far enough."

Priestess felt maybe Guild Girl could have lent her a hand. No, then again, maybe not.

They shared a silent exchange, and then Cow Girl handed her a drink, laughing. "Nice job."

The magical carafe brimmed with cold, pure water. The device had stunned even Priestess, let alone Cow Girl, when they first saw it, but this was no time to be shocked.

"Thank you," Priestess said, taking the water and drinking greedily.

"Very nice work," Cow Girl said again, and then she directed her next question at Guild Girl. "I don't know much about the Supreme God's teachings, but they're not...*that*, are they?"

"Certainly not." Guild Girl was brimming with confidence on that point. She puffed out her chest, as if emphasizing the carefully curated body that was the source of that confidence. Even Cow Girl was taken with her attitude, her certainty that she had nothing to be ashamed of. "Rejecting things by constantly invoking the name of justice—it's not that at all." That, she had to admit, was something she had heard from her friend. She smiled bashfully.

She can be very...cute sometimes.

Cow Girl was the tiniest bit jealous, but she decided to stop at simple admiration. "It would kind of stink if we couldn't have festivals anymore. Where would we get all our fun?"

The harvest and grape festivals represented a prayer for abundance, of course, but festivals were also times of joy. If it was wrong to enjoy them, she didn't know what she would do.

"You know," said Priestess, who had finally wetted her lips and throat with the water. She and the other girl—the *real* little sister of the king, who was resting soundly at that moment—were completely different people. "Do you think he even noticed I was pretending?"

§

"GOROGB...?"

The abrupt roar and shock was enough for even the goblins, who spent their days in noise and uproar, to realize something was wrong.

Maybe everyone had finally gotten tired of this stupid job. Here they were, sent to these boring ruins, without so much as a female to pass the time. Granted, the place was much better than the holes in the ground where they usually made their homes, but far be it for the goblins to be satisfied with that. They were envious of the one who ordered them around for being in a nice room. They could easily imagine dragging him down off his high horse—but those imaginings were quickly replaced by what was right in front of them.

Amid dust and debris from within the ruins, they smelled a beautiful smell, a heavenly scent.

An elf!

An elf woman.*!!*

They were like moths to a flame on a dark night.

The goblins completely forgot themselves; they set off running, more than willing to trample their companions on the way out. They would mob her and violate her, that much was certain. And each imagined himself having the greatest pleasure and privilege.

For that purpose and that purpose only, the goblins crowded the hallway into the innermost sanctum, whereupon…

"GAAAAOOOOOOOOOOOOOOONNNNN!!!!!!"

The fearsome roar of a dragon encircled them.

"Forward!"

At that single word of command, an adventurer in grimy armor burst into the open space of the ruins. Even the quickest of the goblins to recover, however, probably didn't register him. The throwing knife took the creature's life silently, mercilessly. It was no proper sword, but it was enough for the likes of a goblin.

"GOORGB?!?!!?"

The demise of their comrade, clawing at his throat as he choked on his own blood, finally alerted the other goblins that there was a problem.

"GOGB?!"

"GGGRGGBO?!!!?"

"Gods! I've seen enough goblins for a lifetime—even an elf lifetime!"

A flash of what seemed like colored wind followed the slayer of goblins into the room, scowling at the horde of greenskins within.

She moved so fast that she could hardly be seen. Three arrows ready in her bow, loosed in an eyeblink—three goblins shot dead.

"Wish we had Protection!"

"I would prefer Holy Light," came a mechanical voice. Goblin Slayer would never let emotions get in the way of slaying goblins.

"Think about this from my perspective! An innocent maiden wants to be as physically far away from these things as possible!" The elf snorted derisively, although somehow still elegantly.

A massive lizardman and a decidedly less massive dwarf followed her in, their movements as different from hers as the clouds are from the mud. Even Goblin Slayer, who went at the head of their party, was no match for a high elf.

"Don't get too eager, Long-Ears!" Dwarf Shaman groaned, scrambling after them. "Not all of us have long legs around here!"

"You need the exercise anyway!"

"Oh, I'm exercisin'!"

Their banter, the same as their kind had shared since the Age of the Gods, sounded pleasant in the heat of battle; Lizard Priest rolled his eyes merrily. Then he cried, "Eeeyah!" His arms, legs, tail, and fangs became living weapons as he whipped them around, slamming them into goblins as he veritably leaped forward.

"It benefits one not to lament what one was not given. Just as I have no desire to embrace a new faith!"

"A compassionate lizardman? Just the thought's enough to make me laugh!" said High Elf Archer.

The adventuring party cut through the green horde like a sword through the grass.

Goblins' strength, however, is not in their nasty little minds but purely in their numbers. In the dim ruins, the monsters poured out of the many branching paths. They smelled blood; they smelled an elf. They would do violence to her, trample her down, take her in victory—such was the only thing in the goblins' heads.

"Oh, for…!" As High Elf Archer ran forward, she suddenly twisted to one side, shooting under her arm behind her.

"GBBORGB?!?!" A goblin who had been about to flank Lizard Priest was caught in midair, his spine pierced; he tumbled to the ground. Dwarf Shaman cut short the last of his twitching with a ruthless stroke of his ax. Then pressed ever forward.

"Doesn't matter about the Earth Mother or who you've got on your side—there's a lot of 'em here, Beard-cutter!"

"And today?" Goblin Slayer casually flung his dagger as he spoke, killing another goblin. "Do you not mind?"

He tossed the question out as readily as his knife, but it was aimed at no one in particular—so High Elf Archer decided to answer.

"You better believe I mind!" she practically howled—although she didn't stop feeling in her quiver for her next bud-tipped arrow. "But today, I'll let you have it!"

"Good." He acted immediately, taking a small bottle from his item pouch and tossing it over his shoulder to Dwarf Shaman. "Light it."

"Got it!" The instant the bottle was in his hands, he grabbed a flint from his bag of catalysts and intoned, *"Dancing flame, salamander's fame. Grant us a share of the very same."*

No sooner had he spoken than a spark lit the wick that fed into the mouth of the bottle. Once it was burning, Dwarf Shaman promptly pitched it into one of the tunnels.

"GORGBB?"

"GGOBBGRGBB!!"

The first goblins to spot the bottle weren't sure what was happening. It came tumbling from ahead of them; they merely picked it up and scoffed at it. That stupid dwarf couldn't even throw straight!

A second later, those goblins were decorating the walls and ceiling of the passageway, and twelve of their companions were blown backward. There was a *boom* that the adventurers could feel in their bones, and the hallway belched dark fire and scorching wind.

"I knew it was bad news when you stocked up on fire powder!" Dwarf Shaman cried. For someone who saved up so much money, their leader, Beard-cutter, also spent liberally. Dwarf Shaman felt a mixture of annoyance and frustration—as well as a bit of joy at this rare opportunity for a nice, big explosion.

He stuck out his hand to catch the next bottle Goblin Slayer tossed to him.

"Only this plan is bad news," Goblin Slayer said with a nod.

"*All* your plans are bad news!" High Elf Archer stood over a goblin that Goblin Slayer had kicked over, shooting the greenskin from point-blank range and then retrieving her arrow. Her shouting was much less elegant than her movements.

Lizard Priest chortled, baring his fangs. "A pleasure it is when supplies are in abundance!" He added that he hoped to be able to use Fusion Blast breath one day. The Earth Mother's staff rattled in his bag—a bag for holding, of course. It was a magic bag that could hold—well, maybe not quite *anything* but far more than you would expect. A friendly, helpful item that most adventurers with a few quests under their belt possessed.

"We should stuff the dwarf in that bag! Then we wouldn't have to worry about whether he can keep up!"

"You can't put living things in the bag! We've had this conversation!"

"Living things? Dwarves are basically rocks!"

Despite the prevalence of such items, none of the members of this party had ever had one before. They hadn't needed it. Nature provided their arrows—as well as sprites. They relied only on themselves. Their cleric, who wasn't present, had been diligently saving her money, thinking about when she might finally obtain one of the storied items. As for their leader, Goblin Slayer...

"It would be a gruesome prospect if the goblins took it."

And there you had it. It was enough to make High Elf Archer want to take a break from shooting goblins to put her hands to her face or look up at the ceiling. "You heard the man," she said. "Try not to drop it!" She resisted the impulse, instead nocking four arrows into her bow before unleashing them into four goblin heads, literally firing every direction at once. "If you drop it and that thing gets away from us, our names are mud!"

"But of course! I understand."

"It's happened to me before."

"GBBOGB?!"

"GOOGB! GOOBBGRGB?!"

The goblin to the right had procured a spear somewhere, but Goblin Slayer simply battered him. The goblin on the other side, he parried with his shield.

He left that monster for others to deal with, instead picking up the club it had dropped. It would be more helpful than the broken spear. He swung the club mechanically, then flung it forward.

"GBOGB?!" cried a goblin as the club cracked its skull open.

"We've been able to bring down their numbers," he said calmly.

"And I'm sure you're very happy about it!" High Elf Archer said, matching him step for step specifically so she could come up along-side him and give him an annoyed look. "Do you realize these are extremely valuable ruins?!"

"I am aware." Goblin Slayer nodded. "If I didn't understand their construction, I wouldn't do this."

Before, escape had been difficult; they hadn't had enough time.

And what about now?

If only he could ask their priestess for Holy Light... No, maybe he could have their dwarf use Tunnel to create an escape route.

Even without the bag for holding, Lizard Priest was strong enough that he could carry copious quantities of fire powder.

No...

Enough thinking. Goblin Slayer turned his helmeted head from side to side, checking the passageways, counting the goblins. Yes—this was a goblin hunt. He could do this because the quest giver had brought enough money for supplies.

He would take the actions that would allow him to kill goblins faster, better, to take out more of them. He would fight. When you knew the layout of a set of ruins ahead of time, you simply had to charge ahead. Was that not all there was to it?

What about that could be considered an adventure?

He had his friends—even in his own mind, it took him a second to think of them that way—with him.

Therefore, he should focus on what he could do.

For this was a goblin hunt, and he was Goblin Slayer.

"The bulk of them are coming from the left. There aren't many on the right. But there are indeed quite a few of them."

"The forces of Chaos are feeling feisty today!" Lizard Priest cried, even as he kicked back the goblins who pressed in from every direction. For they did swarm indeed; if he slowed down, he would be swallowed up. You didn't have to be High Elf Archer—even an ordinary adventurer would feel they had seen enough goblins right here.

Everyone in this chamber, however, had seen that many and more already in their lives.

"All of which implies they've got a leader!" Dwarf Shaman said as he met a goblin who came flying out of the forked passage with the blade of his ax. He had used more spells—and Lizard Priest more miracles—than usual; Lizard Priest having used two or three and himself two spells.

By the gods, I hate having to conserve my magic!

"Is their leader a goblin, too?" High Elf Archer wondered.

"No."

The elf leaped past a goblin, not even turning around as she shot an arrow through his skull. Another goblin reached for her as she jumped, only to be dispatched when Goblin Slayer kicked him in the neck.

"I doubt that goblins by themselves could have reached the inner chamber of a shrine guarded by the royal family," Goblin Slayer said.

"A reasonable deduction," Lizard Priest agreed, rolling his eyes merrily as he bathed in a shower of goblin blood. He took the corpse of the creature he had torn open, tossing one half of it to each side, then threw himself forward.

Battle was good, but goblin hunting was not enough to be really satisfying. If there was something else waiting for them, though—if these were merely foot soldiers—then that was another story.

They had a commander. A proper leader. There lay glory, there lay merit. It was not something to be thrown away in the sand.

"Friends, comrades! This is our moment to do the deeds for which we will be remembered!" Lizard Priest cried.

"If I lived a century with you, I doubt I'd ever quite get used to the way you think about this stuff…," High Elf Archer said, running along the tail Lizard Priest extended as if it were a branch. "Thanks!" she chirped as she landed back on the stone floor and continued running. "I think you could pick up elf manners sooner than that!"

"I'm afraid I doubt that they would quite suit me!"

"Yeah, that's a problem all right!" High Elf Archer giggled, the bracing sound out of place in this goblin hideout.

They were not letting their guard down, and they weren't full of hubris. If they could have won by stewing in silent anxiety, they would have done so. Instead, they struck a balance between being too stiff and being too relaxed. Only by maintaining that balance would they survive.

This was knowledge they had gained by emerging alive from adventures great and small.

It was only natural—since they were so different from one another. And him? There were things that needed to be spoken and things that needn't be.

"Keep going—forward!" Goblin Slayer said. "Forward!"

Yes, forward—ever on.

He never prayed to the gods. He didn't really know how. Those who could pray were amazing to him.

Which was precisely why now, at this moment, he sought Ruta's protection. The blessing of the god who valued people trying, failing, and trying again to find a better way, a faster way, a more *right* way.

None of the adventurers here could miss the fell presence that loomed in the darkness.

§

He—if that is the proper word—opened his eyes to a terrible racket. He was not in a good mood.

How could he be when his sleep had been interrupted?

What he especially detested, though, were the uncouth noises that came unbidden into his consciousness.

For example, yes—the adventurers' footsteps. Did they know no restraint?

He did not much like the goblins' ruckus, either—but well, that was the way goblins were. One had to accept it. One could be angry that the goblins didn't know how to shut up and hold their places, but there was not much to be done about it.

Adventurers, however—they were different. They were so rude as to come into someone's place of rest, make all this racket, and try to steal their treasure.

Adventurers! Violent ruffians, that's all they are.

Thus he opened the lid of his place of rest in high dudgeon.

"…What, pray tell, is happening out here?" he asked.

"GBG! GOBBGRGB!!" replied a goblin who happened to be in the sleeping chamber—presumably either running away or avoiding work. The creature seemed to be gibbering some sort of excuse.

"I see." He nodded. *I should have known! Goblins—no more useful as lookouts than they are as security.* "Very well. Repulse them immediately—that's all adventurers deserve."

"GRGBGB! GOBBGBOGRG!"

"What are you still doing here? I'm telling you to get going—don't you understand that?"

"GORGB…"

The creature scrambled out of the room with a mixture of fear and contempt and a poorly disguised glare. Ugh. Goblin *attitudes.*

It wasn't the fact of what the monster thought he would do to his master if given half a chance. It was that he thought he would ever even *get* half a chance. It was an insult—a slap in the face!

And from that perspective…

From that perspective, the adventurers were no different from goblins themselves.

"Hmm…"

The idea was a most amusing one. If adventurers and goblins were the same, then they could be dealt with in the same way. Beaten, battered, broken of spirit, made to know that they were inferior life-forms.

Simple discipline, that's what it is. He began to put on some moldy-smelling clothes, one sleeve at a time—one must look decent. *If they'd only kept to themselves, instead of forcing their way into a place they'll never see again, I would have left them alone.*

Goblins were too stupid to understand that—as were adventurers.

"Very well. There is just one thing to do." He smiled. "Teach the adventurers a lesson."

The smile showed bestial fangs in a bloodred mouth.

CHAPTER 4

ROCK YOU!

"We're next, right?" Rhea Fighter asked.

"How many times are you going to ask that?" Wizard Boy replied in annoyance, and he looked away awkwardly.

"This is, what? The fifth time? Sixth?" she said.

"You're counting…?" *Then stop asking*, he wanted to say, but he forced the words down. Instead, he grumbled, "Yeah, we're next."

"…Right."

She nodded, looking serious. She was in the room the swordfighters had been given to prepare. The hall had been opened for the knights who were the center of the tournament, and she and her friend had been given one of the rooms.

Far overhead was the battlefield, whence the cheering of the crowd sometimes shook their room. Why was it so hot? Was that to get the combatants in a fighting mood? Or was it just his own nerves?

Gah… Dammit…

That probably explained it. Why he was so mad. Wizard Boy scratched his head in frustration.

It was only a short break, but taking off your armor was so much more revitalizing than leaving it on.

"…"

Yes, there was a good reason for it, but it still meant there was a girl his own age right next to him...with no armor on. Of course he would sweat a little.

He tried to keep the arcing silhouette of her figure, which her clinging, sweat-soaked underarmor made very visible, out of his line of sight.

That's not the point.

He knew what she was focusing on. And because he knew, he was a jerk for trying to get in her way.

A jerk and stupid.

He'd become an adventurer precisely so he could stick it to the people who pointed at him and laughed. So the last thing he wanted was to do anything that would make him like them.

Still, the soft warmth beside him, rising and falling, impinged on his consciousness whether he wanted it to or not.

"You had a drink, right?" he asked in hopes of distracting himself. His voice was sharp.

"Yeah, I did," the rhea girl said in a way that suggested her mind was elsewhere. She leaned against the back of her chair, then kept leaning until the chair started to tilt over. The movement sent some drops running down her pale throat, drawing new lines across the underarmor of her chest. "So we're next, right?"

"Listen, you...," Wizard Boy started, although even he wasn't sure what he planned to say. His mouth was still open when he was rescued by a gentle knock at the door.

"...Hmm?"

"Hoh."

They moved as one; Wizard Boy grabbed his staff and touched the boomerang at his hip as he rose from his seat. He went to the door with True Words bubbling in the back of his mind, approaching not straight on but from the side.

"Who's there?" he called.

"Inspector of the field. Mind if I come in?"

I know that voice.

Wizard Boy let out a relieved breath and opened the door—then stared in surprise.

"Hey! Working hard?"

"Oh! You're the girl from the farm!" the rhea exclaimed.

Wizard Boy didn't say anything but made way for Cow Girl. She had red hair, she was tall, and perhaps most troubling of all, she was *very* well-endowed. What's more, today she was dressed in the capital's latest fashion. Everything about her, from her outfit to her attitude, seemed different from usual.

I never know what to do with her…, Wizard Boy thought, letting out a breath. For she was, when you got right down to it, a woman who minded her appearance.

"Here you go—some provisions. Good luck!"

"Whoopee!"

Even as Wizard Boy was busy ruminating, the girls seemed to be having fun. Rhea Fighter took the basket Cow Girl had brought, tossing her hands in the air and shouting with delight.

Rheas ate five or six times a day—which took time, making the interval between battles that much shorter.

It wasn't fair…

He resisted the thought. It wasn't unconditionally true. *For starters, what did it mean to be fair in light of the particular qualities of a living thing?* the boy wondered. Rheas might not have much stamina, but they were extremely quick over short stretches—and they had an ability to *digest* that far outstripped humans. If you could store up heat very quickly and use it to move, maybe that actually gave you an advantage, in a way.

Won't know unless I try…

"Do what you need to do, but try not to stuff yourself," he said.

"Yep!" the rhea girl answered, her mouth already full.

Wizard Boy looked in the basket and found sandwiches consisting of dried meat and pickled vegetables stuffed between pieces of bread.

A light human lunch would be little more than a snack for a rhea. No problem, then. At least it wouldn't make it hard for her to move…

"Hmm?"

He realized she was used to this. As he tried studiously to avoid looking at the rhea girl in her moderately clothed state, his eyes met Cow Girl's instead. The older woman gave him a questioning look, at which he shook his head and said, "Nothing. He here?"

©Noboru Kannatuki

His words were brusque and brief, but Cow Girl understood what he meant and nodded. "Yeah, he's here."

"That right?"

"Not here with me, though," she mumbled, sounding a little lonely.

The boy felt a rush of frustration. This was *him* they were talking about. There was a nine out of ten chance—really, infinitely closer to ten—that he was off somewhere at that moment…

…*hunting goblins.*

It had to be, knowing him.

"……"

The rhea, her mouth full of bread, looked at Wizard Boy, and then her eyes went wide. "I know!" she said, and a catlike grin spread across her face. "You wanted him to *see* us!"

"I did not!" Wizard Boy shot back, his voice cracking. It made him feel dumb—he was as good as telling her she was right. He coughed once. "I mean, stuff like this… You don't do it so that people can watch you."

He stood up again, thoroughly disgusted. The feeling he had was, well, not unlike wanting to be complimented. He couldn't completely deny the desire for recognition that burned within him.

It was like a bucket with a hole in it. Pour water in, and it would just run out again. There was never enough. There never could be.

Would it have been different if his sister were there? These days, he felt like he didn't even know that.

For one thing…

"I'm not the star here. She is."

He hated the idea of using someone who was working so hard for his own advantage.

The rhea girl looked at him with an expression that was hard to describe—part embarrassed, part guilty, part disappointed. It was a very complicated look indeed.

"Hmm," Cow Girl said, and then she leaned down and added, "Hey…"

"Huh?" Rhea Fighter looked up at her.

"That stuff he said before the joust started—that was pretty cool, wasn't it?"

"Oh!" The rhea caught on immediately, swinging her arms with maybe a little too much enthusiasm and exclaiming, "Yeah, it was totally awesome! No one's ever talked about me like that before, ever!"

Wizard Boy produced an inarticulate sound halfway between a grunt and groan and looked away. After all, it was obvious what they were doing. He was humiliated to think they were expecting such things of him.

It was like they were trying to talk a child into doing something— except that to dismiss them out of hand would have been the most childish thing of all.

"For that matter, I think this is the first time anyone has even cheered me on while I was fighting. It really makes you think, like, *Yeah! I can do this!*"

Just listen to her.

She could exclaim about how awesome something was without a second thought and really mean it. Wizard Boy glared at her.

"Doesn't that make it pretty much like magic?" she asked.

Finally, he sighed a great sigh. He surrendered. He had lost.

"...Fine. The two of us together, then—that sound good?"

"Sounds great!" Rhea Fighter nodded enthusiastically. Then suddenly, her expression changed, and she said, "Oh, but—"

Rheas were always like this. Always completely absorbed in whatever was going on around them. It was something of a saving grace for Wizard Boy, who was given to worry.

"—don't you think it's about time you helped me into my armor?"

"Pbbt...?!"

It was, however, also the seed of much personal danger.

He scowled, but she ignored him. "You see?" she said. "He never helps me with it! Even though it's so much work!"

"Ah..." Cow Girl scratched her cheek, not quite sure what to say. When she thought of her old friend, she somehow felt like maybe she could sort of almost nearly understand. "I guess that's just how boys are."

"Listen, you...!"

§

High Elf Archer didn't bother thinking too hard as she poured arrows on the mass of encroaching goblins. She'd already learned long ago (she chuckled at herself for thinking of it that way): This was no adventure.

That didn't stop her acute elven senses from picking up on even the slightest change, her ears twitching. "Does the air seem different somehow...?" she asked.

"Perhaps."

She shot the nearest goblin in the head, pulled the arrow out, and put it right back in her bow before shooting another one with it, farther away. Goblin Slayer pressed forward, paying no attention to what a luxury it was to be able to effectively ignore the astonishing archery of a high elf.

The goblins moved up to try stopping him.

"GBRG!"

"GRG! GOOGBGR!!"

They've started to become more orderly.

Still, there couldn't be even a hundred of them. He plunged a sword through the throat of his twenty-fifth goblin, then kicked the corpse away.

"GOBBG?!"

If there's one way in which humans are quantifiably superior to goblins, it's reach. Simply having longer arms and legs means being able to maintain a greater distance. Ahead of the goblins, farther away from the goblins. As long as you kept that in mind...

...then we can deal with this number somehow.

He remembered the times he had explored with the boy—in the tower, in a dungeon. This was not as bad as those times.

When goblins were piling in from all sides, there was only one thing to do. Cut a path ahead.

The threat of goblins did not lie in their nastiness but only in their numbers. As long as the party could avoid getting surrounded and maintain their vitality—not their HP, mind you—there would be no problem.

Although he would be loath to have to do the same thing on open ground.

"Arrows!"

"Right."

As such, the only real issue was which weapons to throw and what to replace them with. Goblin Slayer pulled out a dagger tucked amid his armor and flung it at a goblin hiding by a pillar, killing him. He used the momentum to leap forward, vaulting toward the goblin and grabbing its quiver, which he tossed through the air. Neither did he forget the goblin's specialty—a rusty sword, which he kicked up into his hand.

"Thanks!" High Elf Archer's lithe arm stretched out, catching the arcing quiver, and that was a relief. There's nothing more unnerving than an empty quiver. Even goblin arrows are better than no arrows at all.

"You're very high maintenance, Long-Ears!"

"I prefer the term *civilized*!" High Elf Archer shot back, sending a snorting laugh in the direction of Dwarf Shaman, who was busy cracking a goblin's skull open with his ax. "Unlike certain hole dwellers!"

"Hoh! At least we're smart enough to stay out of the rain, unlike the elves!"

Goblin Slayer moved ahead, flinging the rusty sword at another goblin and killing him while High Elf Archer and Dwarf Shaman argued nearby. Arrows rained down in every direction, while Dwarf Shaman's ax did its own talking on his behalf.

With them helping to hold the goblins at bay, Lizard Priest had some breathing room. "A swamp can be quite a nice place as well, you know!" he said as he used his superlative tail to slam a goblin to its death against a wall—a literal rear guard.

Naturally, he hesitated to defile the holy staff with goblin blood. The statue, however, was another matter.

The goblins were never going to stop Lizard Priest with nothing but a little horde. Which meant rather than having him up front, it was better to use him to broaden their vision. After all, they were one cleric short this evening.

"What do you think?" Goblin Slayer asked.

"I think they've started to become more orderly," Lizard Priest replied, echoing the judgment of the man who at that moment was relieving a throatless goblin of its club. "I believe we can presume that whoever is commanding them is cognizant of the situation and has begun taking measures to respond."

"With this scale, I doubt it's a goblin lord," Goblin Slayer said, swinging his club to the right and muttering "Twenty-eight" under his breath. "However, I don't think goblins would follow a shaman so obediently."

"GBBG?!"

"Some servant of Chaos, then. A dark elf? A cultist? Perhaps some worshipper of evil spirits? Or…"

"GORG! GGORB?!"

"GBOBGR?!"

Their conversation was punctuated by the screams of dying goblins. Not that they noticed.

High Elf Archer frowned at the spraying blood, but a second later, her ears were twitching. "Up ahead! Something's coming!"

"Hrm…!"

At that moment, a red light pierced the darkness. No sooner had they registered the beam than it was already passing by, impossible to evade. Without the high elf's senses to alert him, it would have sliced Goblin Slayer clean in half. Then again, he had never been under the impression that his armor would stop anything but a goblin attack.

Let alone a lord of darkness such as advanced now from the shadows.

"The hell is that thing?!" Dwarf Shaman cried.

"At the very least, it's not a goblin," his leader replied, stating the obvious.

No, it was no goblin—it was sheer menace, as if the darkness itself had taken on form. It wasn't just Goblin Slayer who didn't recognize it—hardly anyone would. But anyone would know to be afraid.

If Priestess had been there—or perhaps Harefolk Hunter or even Club Fighter or the cleric of the Supreme God. If one of them had been there, they might have recognized it. There was a freezing chill like terror. It was not hatred nor greed but rather the pride and murderous disinterest of a being that viewed living things as nothing more than cattle.

There stood a man with pallid skin. His slick red lips opened, and a bizarre voice issued forth:

"You would speak of me in the same breath as goblins? There are insults one cannot bear…"

It was almost like he was talking to himself, like they shouldn't have been able to hear him, and yet the voice reached the adventurers.

The man's skin might have been pale, but his eyes burned in the darkness. At first glance, he appeared young. He wasn't dressed in anything so silly as evening wear. He was a warrior, and his armor seemed patterned on a skinned animal, a gruesome dark red, as if some creature had been turned inside out to put the innards on display.

A great many words existed for this creature, this being: the clan of darkness. Nosferatu. The walking undead. All words invented to describe these monsters.

As the old poet Byron said:

But first, on earth as vampire sent,
Thy corse shall from its tomb be rent:
Then ghastly haunt thy native place,
And suck the blood of all thy race;
There from thy daughter, sister, wife,
At midnight drain the stream of life;
Yet loathe the banquet which perforce
Must feed thy livid living corse:
Thy victims ere they yet expire
Shall know the demon for their sire,
As cursing thee, thou cursing them,
Thy flowers are withered on the stem.

"Vampire!" High Elf Archer screamed.

§

Had the field of combat ever fallen completely quiet until this moment?

The people in the packed grandstands, from every corner of the capital, stared down in mute amazement. The silence was enough to make your ears hurt. Finally, one thing resounded through it: the clopping of hooves.

Surely there had never been in all the Four-Cornered World a donkey who stepped so proudly. If there had been one, perhaps it was Dapple, the beloved mount belonging to the servant of that knight with his mournful countenance.

What was more: Behold the hero who rode astride that animal. Sword by side, shield in hand, lance by elbow, a knight as fine as any in the sagas. Armor of the purest white, like unblemished snow, helmet crowned with wings of white as well.

Peeking out from beneath the helmet's raised visor was the face of a blushing, sweet, but quite gutsy young woman. Her small body, tucked inside all that armor, was soft and delicate and beautiful—though few knew it.

Yet one only had to look in order to learn.

The entire place waited with bated breath for the moment when she would draw the lovely tempered steel within the elegant white scabbard.

She was a bud, someone said. The bud of a white rose. She was in that one fleeting instant before she bloomed in her pride.

No one recalled the mirth to which she had been subject when she first appeared in the coliseum only a few days before. No one remembered snickering at the rhea girl's modest size and unimpressive form.

As they all focused upon her now, no one suspected…

He was all upset because he thought I would find out he was practicing his painting!

…that she had completely the wrong idea about what had happened.

Regardless, the rhea girl felt her heart pounding with every step her donkey took—indeed, it had been since the moment she left the greenroom. She felt it jump with each clop of the hooves. Her whole body felt itchy. But she smiled.

It had started the moment the wizard boy had painted her armor with some magic paints. He'd meant to save them for the finals, he said—but he'd decided to use them now.

He waved his brush in the air, and her helmet had become striking, her armor had become wonderful—and somehow, it made her feel as if she had become wonderful, too. If she hadn't been sitting in the saddle already, she would have jumped up and hugged him.

She no longer felt nervous; instead, she buzzed with excitement. She squinted at the knight across the field, eager to go.

I've made it this far. You'll see what I can do!

"Why, in that armor, she hardly looks like a rhea at all! You've made her a display piece. It's disrespectful to her!" groaned the paladin of the Supreme God, whose voice had, until a moment before, been lost in the thunderous applause of the crowd.

He wasn't looking at the girl, sitting upon her trusty mount. Well, he *was* looking at her, but in the same way that one might look at a stone on the side of the road.

"The rules regarding armor will have to be tightened up. This tournament is a disaster. And worst of all…"

For the first time, he seemed to really look at something. His eyes swept upward, toward the royal box. The king was nowhere to be seen, but his sister was sitting there, wearing a gorgeous white dress. She was waving reluctantly, first to the crowds and then to the knights on the battlefield.

Behind her stood two women, dressed in the latest fashions and all but expressionless. One of them looked entirely proud of her attractiveness, while the other was making no effort at all to hide her ample bosom. The knight glared at them as if they were the most despicable kind of evil, then slowly shook his head.

"…I swear, I can't stop shaking." He literally spat the words, then lowered his visor and secured the fastener.

It didn't really matter, though. The rhea was watching her opponent only in order to win. For herself. Not for him.

She touched her own visor, then stopped and looked back with… was that hope?

"…"

She saw the wizard boy standing there.

He was fiddling with his small staff, touching the boomerang at his hip, looking around and grumbling. To any outside observer, he would simply have looked anxious—but Rhea Fighter knew. This was how he acted when he was busy thinking of something to help her. She didn't understand the more arcane aspects of what he did—but it was all she needed to know.

"…Hey," he said when he noticed her looking. That was all, a brief sound of affirmation.

So she replied, "Right!" and lowered her visor with a *clank*.

I've come this far. All that's left is to do it…

Wizard Boy watched her go; as she rode toward the list, she seemed at once like both the smallest and the biggest presence on the field.

"Do—or don't! There's no try!" he remembered the nasty old rhea bellowing at him. But yeah—he was right. You couldn't *try* killing goblins. You couldn't *try* slaying a dragon. That just wasn't how it worked.

As that faraway paladin had proved, it was the choice to *do* that enabled one to overcome a dragon.

Even the stupidest burglar wouldn't just *try* to filch a gem from a dragon's treasure hoard.

Screw it, the boy thought as he watched the girl go. He took in a breath, as if he was breathing in everything in the world along with it. Spells? The hell with 'em.

Just look at the great sorcerers. They showed that *not* using magic put it on an even higher level.

What he needed? He already had it all. The silence. More eloquent than any words. Thus, he drew another breath.

Just watch me, you old shithead. You could never do this. Just hurry up and die. Like my sister.

Imagining that bastard with his crusty laugh was here in this very stadium, the boy yelled:

"Those who are far, listen with your ears! Those who are near, see with your eyes!"

His voice projected. There were no spells. No clever tricks. Magical paints? Oh, please. It was high noon—they had the sun. This battlefield. The spectators were looking from far away. He'd just painted it white, polished it, and stuck on some wings. That was all—no magic involved.

They didn't need it to do this. Not him—and not her.

You got a problem? You want to make an issue of it? Go ahead, bitch away!

*   *   *

"The younger brother of Ruby Mage, formerly the first sorcerer of the Academy, now speaks!"

That set off a murmur among part of the crowd. At least, he thought so. He couldn't tell. Maybe he was imagining it.

Doesn't matter! Like I care!

It wouldn't mean the end of anything. He knew that. He knew that all too well.

They would probably keep talking about it for a long time. In his own heart, he felt a shadow, one that wouldn't let go.

But so what, then?

The old rhea had spoken often and eloquently of the greatest of the sorcerers, of what had made him such a fine user of magic. Fools said that it was because he spoke with dragons, because he retrieved treasure, because he had crossed the border between life and death.

But it was none of that. It was because he—he himself was...

"The adventurer—my friend!"

...because he had accepted his own shadow. He had a friend who had offered him that chance—that was what made the great sorcerer great.

If so, then this was Wizard Boy's first step. He would take it for her sake—she was the one who had caused him to take it. Maybe people would say he lacked courage not to be able to say these things to her face—but what did he care?

It doesn't matter. I'll do it!

"The rhea fighter, unparalleled, invincible! Of her brave deeds and her beauty, you have surely all heard by now!"

True, the shadow clung to him and refused to loosen its grip. True, he would travel with the shadow wherever he went, wherever it might be.

He couldn't overcome it. And he felt a repulsion at the idea of accepting it—only the sages were capable of such things.

So long as he couldn't, though, he would have to drag himself along, pathetically buffeted this way and that. To despise that patheticness and to seek only the glory of the light would be as absurd as burying himself in darkness.

For going to such extremes was as good as admitting you couldn't look squarely at the other side.

"And why? Surely you know these words, spoken since before the journey of the nine walkers!"

If they didn't? Well, it just showed they hadn't studied enough. Read a book! Learn something! Then go out into the world, go on a journey, have an adventure.

No? They couldn't? What did he care? There was only *do*. After all, look: *She* was here, doing it.

She'd left her rural home, become an adventurer in spite of the mockery, trained hard, and was on a journey now. She was here at this moment. And she'd brought him along with her.

Yeah, that was right. You say this wasn't the fruits of his own labor? Well, that's true. He hadn't done it on his own.

He understood now. He knew very well. Rheas? Rheas were...

"Rheas are the race who looks up!"

And that wasn't all—no, not in the least. Race didn't determine everything.

It was the first thing some people noticed, and they thought it made someone good or bad, strong or weak. They would make fun of someone for it!

But race didn't determine everything about a person. He gestured toward the young woman in white with one arm.

"And she is a great adventurer!"

Not she *will be* a great adventurer. She already was. She was already fully fledged and more. After all, none of the other rheas from her shire were here. And the other sorcerers from the Academy were in the spectator seating, not on the field.

"One day, this battle shall be one act of her legend! Therefore..."

The young woman, and she alone, had come this far—had brought him this far.

"Therefore, I shall forbear to say any more. Except for one word: her name!"

Then, at the top of his voice, the boy pronounced the rhea girl's name.

Godspeed!

This last, he wished her only in his heart.

"———————————————————!!!!"

Applause like thunder. People cheered her name, making it ring around the stadium.

She looked about, almost as if she was confused—and then she raised her hands high. If the earlier cheering had not been enough to pierce the very tent tops, now it was like the thunder was accompanied by lightning that crashed down to the field of battle.

"Eep!" she yelped, startled, but then she started laughing, a proper guffaw, and thrust her fist into the air once more.

As for the knight who waited across from her...

"......"

He sat dumbfounded upon his horse. No doubt in the world he lived in, rheas were poor little creatures deserving of sympathy—but no more. Perhaps he himself deserved a good word for her arrival in this place.

She was a true, unfettered, unblemished knight.

But what do I care?

"How do you like that?" Wizard Boy was looking his way with a brazen, incongruous smile. "There's your fairness and equality."

§

"Darn it! This isn't fair!"

High Elf Archer's shout was drowned out by the roar as two monsters charged toward her. The ancient shrine, which should have been the sanctuary of the Earth Mother, was now the site of a desperate battle.

A fearsome descendant of the nagas kicked aside the goblins mobbing him, then went after the man in red-black armor.

"Eeeeeyaahhh!"

"You call that an attack?!"

There was an audible *crack* as sword met claws. Sparks flew, the hot, red flashes illuminating both combatants.

It was *not* a contest, this matching of prodigious strengths. Lizard Priest swung his claws, fangs, and tail with everything he had, the claws of his feet scraping as they slid across the floor. He was only keeping his opponent at bay—even he, who had gone toe to toe with a red dragon.

"A descendant of the fearsome nagas has entered my stronghold? Oh, how the mighty have fallen!"

"Is it so? They say my forebears could see in the dark!"

Keeping the opponent at bay was nothing to be ashamed of. Lizard Priest howled again and traded another set of blows with the vampire. A single stroke from the Earth Mother's staff might have been effective, but having come so far—it wasn't that he wouldn't use it but that he couldn't. If his opponent grabbed hold of it during their exchange, he would have no way to fight back; it would be taken from him. Then they would be back to square one. These experienced, hardened adventurers were not going to make such a foolish mistake.

Which was precisely why...

"There...!"

High Elf Archer didn't miss a beat; she kicked off the walls of the ruins to get some height and then let her arrows fly. They were pitiful goblin arrows but fired by a sublime archer. Wielded by a high elf, they might as well have been magic missiles.

Which is to say, they were inerrant, finding their mark even when the target was locked in combat, the rusty old arrowheads burying themselves in the vampire.

"That tickles!"

"Oh, for—! You'd think he was some kind of ogre!"

It was bad enough to have your arrows deflected with a flourish of the sword, but to have them simply picked out after they'd hit their target—that was a bit much.

Despite their poor state, the arrows had bitten deep, but the vampire didn't begrudge a bit of torn flesh as he pulled them out. Dark, rotten blood flowed forth but only for a second. The next moment, the flesh bubbled up and closed the wounds.

High Elf Archer flew through space, watching it happen with almost divine vision; she bit her lip.

Unfortunately, they had more to worry about than just the vampire.

"GGGGG…"

"BB…"

Goblins. No—not quite.

They were something that had once been goblins.

Their skulls had been crushed, their throats torn out, their innards pierced—and yet they stood. Rose. Returned from the dead. As the vampire's miasma touched them, first one and then another got to its feet.

This—this was the power of the Death, the special privilege of the Dungeon Master. The very same thing that had tormented those heroes of the forces of Order as they faced the Army of Darkness.

"BRAAINN…"

"BBBRRRRRAAAAAIN…"

The moment Lizard Priest moved to attack the vampire, the party's fighting strength was hampered.

"I've got you!"

When even High Elf Archer had to move to reinforce him, it seemed the end was at hand. She perched on a stone pillar, literally raining arrows upon the unholy horde that now defiled the Earth Mother's sanctuary.

One, two, five, ten. The goblin corpses piled up again in the blink of an eye. It was an important act of reinforcement for the adventurers— if nothing else, it bought them a second to breathe.

But only a second. For an instant later, the creatures creaked and twisted and rose again like broken puppets hauling themselves to their feet.

"Never gonna see the end of 'em at this rate!" Dwarf Shaman said in between strokes of his ax.

"That's normal," was Goblin Slayer's reply. He had never known a battle with goblins to have a proper end. The only limit was how many of them there were in a given place.

But these are not goblins.

He tried stabbing one in the throat with a dagger, as he so often did, only to have it shiver and continue after him. He beat it back with his shield, gaining himself enough time to reposition.

When a creature comes back from the dead, its brain is rotted, so it's unable to form proper thoughts. Considerable devotion and study are required to become a superior form of this sort of life, like the vampire.

Which is to say, goblins could not become vampires.

All that was left to the shambling corpses was their greed—although in that sense, they weren't so different from when they had been alive.

Goblin Slayer didn't know the first thing about the undead—but he was getting the idea, just by comparing these creatures to their living counterparts. There were two major differences. One was that, of the major biological needs, only hunger remained.

The other was that, apparently, stopping them took more work than usual.

"What should we do?" he asked.

"Get it so they can't move!" Dwarf Shaman yelled. He was busy wielding his weapon, trusting to his people's natural strength to get the job done. It would have been great to use a spell, if they could—but *were* there any spells that would work on a vampire? Playing one of your all-too-limited cards in an uncertain situation would show if not a lack of nerve at least a lack of forethought.

Dwarves have their own way of fighting. Dwarf Shaman wasn't done yet. And so he chopped the spinal cord of one of the corpses like a log.

"Arms and legs!" he called. "Or the spine! That'll do, too!"

"Understood."

With the decision made, Goblin Slayer acted quickly. He didn't know how to destroy a zombie—but he knew many, many ways to destroy goblins.

Moreover...

If only the girl was here.

Then they could have hit the creatures with Holy Light and started carving a path through the stunned monsters or perhaps used Purify to take care of them all in one swoop.

Under his metal helmet, he grunted at the thought, then took out his annoyance on a goblin corpse.

In other words, he kicked it down, he smashed its spinal cord underfoot, and he stole the club from its hands.

"There's no point counting anymore," he said. Faced with the dead pressing in from every side, what was the benefit in knowing how many you had destroyed?

Especially when those dead creatures were goblins. Then the goal was simply to survive.

A club. That's the weapon for moments like these.

Goblin Slayer struck out with the club, right and left, trusting to luck to land his blows. Each time he sent a goblin corpse flying, creating a small space, he would immediately step into it, working his way forward. Bereft of the premise that death meant stillness, he knew he had to get out of this large room.

I will never fight with goblins in an open space again.

He remembered—it had been back in year one for him. How he had struggled to protect a village. Thinking back on it, he knew his performance had been pathetic, but still, he had learned much from it. It had become part of his experience. Confined spaces were his bread and butter—although even that could vary with time and occasion.

"Orcbolg! Wind direction!"

The party members he had gained since then were better than he was at other things besides hunting goblins. The elf, whom he'd known for years now, felt the instantaneous change, her acute sensory receptors catching the movement of the wind sprites.

She pointed. He peered into the darkness from behind his visor—and there, he was sure, was a passage.

"That way!" he said as he split a goblin's head open afresh, trampling over the toppled corpse as he went. "Let's go!"

At the same moment as he shouted, indeed almost in the same breath, he flung his club with a casual motion. It wasn't as fast as the hammer of that famous thunder god nor the flying dagger, but it was the perfect way to kill a goblin.

As the object arced through the air, you would have had to have the vision of a centaur to avoid it. Even with the vampire's monstrous field of view, if he registered it only just before it struck, it was too late. Or perhaps he didn't feel it was worth dodging—but if so, he was wrong.

The club struck the vampire square in the back of the head, cracking his skull open. The bones broke audibly, and the brain made a squishing sound. The insides of the vampire's head came flying out like fireworks.

That single blow gave Lizard Priest ample time to turn—

"Ha! Plain wood!"

Oops. No, it didn't.

The vampire's eyes burned bright even as he mopped up brain matter.

Blast! I don't know what made me think using goblins would be a good idea!

Unbeknownst to the vampire, however, while they had been alive, the goblins had more than fulfilled their role as his shield. If that high elf had had even a single bud-tipped bolt left, it would already have been through his heart.

None here were aware of that fact, however. Not a single one of them.

"I see," Goblin Slayer muttered. "He is indeed a monster."

"Now you understand!" the vampire howled and lashed out with claws that grew from his hand. Perhaps this was the price he paid for his regenerative powers—his bestial, inhuman nature, like a bat or a demon, was made manifest in him.

"Hrrnn…ahhh!"

Lizard Priest struck the ground with his tail, kicking off the stones with his great clawed feet and launching himself into the air. His vestments tore with a *riiiip*, and the dragon fangs he carried as catalysts scattered everywhere.

A hair's breadth: He'd lost crucial resources, but he still had his life. And the magic bag was still safe, too.

Then, well!

In that case, he had nothing to be ashamed of, this descendant of the fearsome nagas—he had only to live!

For the moment, his only task was to avoid follow-up attacks. It would take everything he had. He ducked low to avoid the inevitable blow—but then he blinked his eyes; twice, in fact, on account of his nictitating membranes.

The attack didn't come.

For a second, for the barest instant, the vampire stood stock-still.

"Ahh! Mercy upon the misfortune of the crurotarsi!" Lizard Priest cried. He didn't waste the precious instant in thought but sprung forward with all his terrible force. He cleared the zombies in a single bound, crushing a goblin corpse underfoot as he landed. Even a living goblin couldn't have resisted him.

Death from above. None could measure the awful force and mass of a flying lizardman.

"Are you okay?!" cried High Elf Archer, going pale.

"Indeed—of course!" Lizard Priest chortled, thrusting his long neck forward. "Ahhh, my, my! Perhaps we could call it right here when I have triumphed in a battle of life and death!" Carefully clutching the bag holding the Earth Mother's staff, Lizard Priest rolled up his tail and ran.

"Don't think so," High Elf Archer said, trying to put on a brave face as she darted past him like the wind. "I mean, he was already dead a long time ago, right?"

"Touché!" Lizard Priest bellowed, and then he was with his companions once more.

Goblin Slayer was swinging an iron sword he'd stolen from a goblin, working with Dwarf Shaman to secure the passageway. Lizard Priest dove past them, followed by High Elf Archer, and Dwarf Shaman after her. Last in came Goblin Slayer with his grimy armor, slipping away.

"…Damnable things!" the vampire cursed—almost literally—as he treaded on the white fangs at his feet. The adventurers didn't realize that his eyes had been temporarily fixated on the teeth as they flew through the air. The instant it had taken him to count them—that was the instant that had granted the adventurers their lives.

The vampire *had* to count any scattered objects he encountered. It was an immutable law laid down by the gods. That was simply how vampires worked in the Four-Cornered World. If he rebelled against that stricture, he would no longer be a vampire—he would become nothing but a corpse.

That was how magic functioned. This creature had a monstrous field of vision, and it had only been one instant—but it was enough.

That was the decisive stroke. And what had brought it on? Fate and Chance.

Namely, the adventurers' unremitting effort and force of will had dragged the outcome into being.

§

"Eek!"

There was a sound like splitting logs, and both lances burst into shards of wood. The rhea girl's cry was lost in the crash, and it disappeared before anyone had heard it. Under her visor, though, she flushed red. To scream just because the enemy had struck her!

The brutal shock ran down the left side of her body, nearly throwing her from her saddle. She braced herself in the stirrups and clutched the reins, managing to hold fast. She didn't fall out—excellent. Wait… Was it excellent?

Do you have to ask?!

If she didn't win, there was no point. Her eyes glinted with fighting spirit, and she wheeled her donkey around. There, on the other side of the tilt—there he was. The knight was still on his horse.

The girl shouted, "Points?!"

"One point!" said Wizard Boy, who came scrambling up, clutching a fresh lance. He held it out to her. Within the confines of her visor, she could barely see the flags raised to indicate the number of points. "But thanks to my little oration, the crowd is on our side!"

"So what?!"

"So subjectively, we're even!" Wizard Boy said with a bitter smile. "His lance broke, too, after all."

Rhea Fighter made an angry "hrm" under her helmet.

For a second, the boy thought she was hurt, but then he realized the reaction was emotional.

"What, you upset?" he asked.

"Not *upset*. I'm sure he'll have some kind of excuse."

"Ahhh..."

Like maybe that he'd been going easy on her because she was a rhea. That would be hard to stomach—that much, Wizard Boy could understand.

"I want to win this. On merit. And no questions!"

"Then you'd better really thrash him," the boy said, handing her the lance. He patted her helmet, *plonk*, just once.

"Right!" she said with an energetic nod, and then she leaned forward in the stirrups. She couldn't forget to give her trusty mount a pat on the neck and congratulate him on a job well done. He was working just as hard as she was—he was a mere donkey, and he'd brought her this far against trained warhorses.

We're not gonna lose now!

Filled with fresh determination, the rhea girl readied her lance.

As for the knight, he looked as calm as anything. (Well, not that you could actually tell with his visor down.) He lazily raised his lance toward her, like he didn't care whether he won or not.

I don't like it.

Yeah—the rhea girl didn't like it at all. He'd traded lances, but she didn't *feel* anything from him.

I know I'm not my grandfather, but still.

Her dear departed grandfather, who had gone to the great dungeon under the mountain—he might have sensed the knight's killing impulse or at least his warrior spirit or something. The modest rhea girl, however, hadn't yet reached such a point. But nonetheless...

He thinks I can't do this.

She knew that was what was on her opponent's mind. He thought rheas were poor, small, weak creatures in need of protection. He thought, therefore, that the fact she had come this far was thanks to his own intercession, her victories only an exception to the rule. The hit she'd scored just now would not enter into his consideration—in other words, she wasn't worthy of even thinking about.

Somewhere in there was something almost like compassion. Almost, but not quite.

To be regarded as someone who wasn't even there—now, that made the rhea girl very, very angry.

It was the same way the people of the shire had kept their distance from her as she went around waving her stick, working at being a fighter.

I'm gonna send his ass flying!

It just didn't feel nice.

"Eeeyaaaahh!"

Almost before the judge had waved the flag, she gave a great cry and spurred her mount, launching forward. The jabbering of the spectators disappeared, as did the shouts of the boy wizard behind. Inside the confines of her visor, her vision narrowed to a single point, closing around her opponent.

She gritted her teeth, hefting the weight in her right arm. Her body lurched up. She rose in the saddle.

She braced herself against the stirrups, gripped the reins as hard as she could, made her small self even smaller, and thrust the lance forward.

This was one of the forms she'd used time and time again since the tournament had started.

In any other contest, the result would have been down to her opponent's study of *his* opponent. It was unlikely, however, that the knight was thinking about such things. He was simply too confident: A casual thrust from above, he believed, was the way to deal with small enemies.

As they crossed lances, the girl's eyes went wide. Her lance worked. Her opponent's weapon came closer.

It would be disrespectful to call it the fruit of much training on the knight's part, and it was certainly no mistake by the rhea girl.

It was simply the pips on the dice of Fate and Chance.

"Heeek?!"

There was a metallic crash, and the girl felt herself go flying.

No—she was thrown backward in the saddle like a discarded puppet, but she was still safe. Her feet in the stirrups just held her in place.

The rest of her, however, was in poor shape. The shock was like she'd been hit by a wild animal or a battering ram; the instrument may have been a competition lance, but the blow was still very powerful. Her white-painted armor was battered; the lance had pierced her visor, rendering it useless. If she hadn't had it, she would have been in a fearful state indeed. Then again, even with the visor, there was always that king who had been killed by an errant piece of wood.

With a little less luck—with a critical failure, say—that could have been her fate.

The crowd watched with bated breath for any sign of life from the girl, who sat motionless on her donkey.

Even if she survived, this was a costly outcome. For her breastplate had slipped, revealing her underarmor clinging to her chest for all to see. The curves, intact, moved up and down in time with her breathing, even though she was flat on her back atop her donkey.

She couldn't seem to get a breath. *Huff, huff.* It was just air, moaning in and out through her lips.

The sky... It never looked so blue...

Her head was spinning, her thoughts felt half-formed. Her vision was fuzzy. Past her ruined visor, she saw the boy upside down. He was clenching his fist, trying to keep her from jumping up, shouting something.

"Don't fall off"?

"......!!!"

Then the girl's eyes went wide, as if she'd been struck by lightning, and she clenched her scrupulously built abdominal muscles and sat up in the saddle.

"Hn... Haaah!"

She found a shout at her lips. That was a close one. She shook her head hard. It felt so, so heavy.

Argh!

She tore away the armor that hung limply from her shoulder girdle,

3 45

then reached for her helmet. The visor was warped; she could lift it but barely. She mustered her strength and tore the helmet off her head.

"Hoo!" she exclaimed. She felt like she had been trapped in there for hours, though it had only been a matter of minutes. She shoved aside her hair, stuck to her by the copious sweat on her cheeks and forehead, and sucked in a breath.

A thunderous cheer greeted her safety, and the judge raised a flag in the paladin's corner.

None of that mattered to the girl. She simply waved her fist toward her partner, the boy. He saw her and nodded; she replied with a nod of her own, and then she slapped her cheeks as hard as she could.

Damn! That was a pathetic showing!

If her grandpa or her mentor had seen that, she would never have lived it down. She gritted her teeth from shame, then glared fixedly at her opponent.

The paladin shook his head and muttered, "I knew this very tournament was inherently barbaric..." Did anyone hear him? "It only serves to make rheas and other such peoples the objects of gawkers and to get them hurt as well! It ought to be done away with immediately."

Neither the knight's words nor his opinions would have mattered to most of the people in the stands—and certainly not to the rhea girl.

It started quietly, like a ripple. The yelling and cheering stopped, replaced by mutters of confusion and dismay that slowly built.

It wasn't clear who saw it first—but Rhea Fighter noticed only after Wizard Boy had.

"...Huh?"

She'd turned her mount around for a change of armor—well, not that she had one, but maybe he could swing something—and a fresh lance, to find Wizard Boy pointing upward. At the spectator seating? No, higher than that. The other side of the coliseum?

"The sky...?"

Her gaze rose to the sky she had contemplated a moment earlier. White sunlight pierced the blue. She saw gathering clouds, white and gray, dark and light—and among them, a collection of black smears. As she watched, they grew bigger, until she could see the wings, the claws, the fangs, and the glowing eyes...

"Monsters…?"

The coliseum erupted in screams.

§

"Yah! I flee—for shame!" Lizard Priest howled with uncharacteristic vitriol as he slipped his huge form into the shadow of a pillar. "If the nosferatu are the kings of horror, then the fearsome nagas are the kings of the monsters!"

In spite of his self-censure, he had sustained more than passing injuries. He could endure them because of his great strength and his scales, which gave him an unparalleled ability to carry on in combat.

Satisfied that Lizard Priest's injuries were not going to be a problem, Goblin Slayer said quietly, "It seemed to stop earlier. What did you do?"

"I did nothing. One hears that vampires have a number of weaknesses, however…"

"Don't know much about that," said High Elf Archer as she tied a bandage around Lizard Priest's injuries, knotting it with an elegant motion and speaking as fast as she wrapped. "They're supposed to be weak to sunlight, but you don't get much of that in human temples."

"Why?"

"Because then even the stupidest amateurs would come charging in, thinking they could take care of things, and get themselves bit!" Dwarf Shaman took a swig of his fire wine, shooting a dirty look out past the pillar as he spoke.

Even as zombies—perhaps especially then—the goblins' main menace was in their numbers. However, they moved more slowly, more heavily, with less agility than in life. The vampire didn't seem inclined to send the zombies flying at them. Perhaps it was something to do with his sense of aesthetics.

"You humans have the worst habits," High Elf Archer said, patting the bandaged scales gently and chuckling as she flicked her ears. "You learn one little thing, you think you've got the truth of the whole world figured out."

"I know that all too well," Goblin Slayer said very seriously.

There they were, having a break and a little chat despite the looming army of the dead.

It's often said that adventurers' rest periods can be broken into two kinds, long rests and short ones. Depending on the moment and the situation, a rest might be as little as five minutes—and this was such a time.

This was a party that had always relied minimally on Minor Heal. To revive themselves, they drank stamina potions or snacked on the elven baked goods supplied by their archer.

"Gah. This elvish bread is edible as far as it goes, but it's a little… light," Dwarf Shaman griped. Somewhat lacking as an accompaniment for wine." He picked a few crumbs out of his beard. "I could wish for a roast chicken!"

"Don't like it? Then don't eat it!" High Elf Archer said, licking the crumbs off her fingers and somehow still looking elegant at the same time. "I can't help wishing the girl was here. She's dealt with a vampire before."

"Yes." Goblin Slayer poured the contents of a small bottle through the slats of his visor, then nodded. "She told me the same. Although she wouldn't speak much of it." Next, he whispered, "She is a far more accomplished adventurer than me." This was tinged with gladness as each person there could hear.

If Priestess had been with them at that moment…

"Our cleric is not given to bragging nor accustomed to effusive praise." She would certainly have been pleased. Lizard Priest's eyes spun merrily in his head. Then he stretched, twisting his neck to check how he was feeling after the first aid. "I do believe this occasion will become valuable experience."

"That vampire's the blamed problem!" said Dwarf Shaman, who was seated in a lotus posture as if meditating. He rested his chin on his fist and looked very perturbed. "Don't think you are I are made to take out the likes of that shitkicker, Beard-cutter." He took another long gulp of wine, then fixed Goblin Slayer's helmet with a stare. "You can't be tellin' me you don't know about *vampires* now. I won't believe it!"

"I know of them," Goblin Slayer replied with a nod. "But not much."

"Well, that's a relief!" High Elf Archer said, half in exasperation, half in amusement. "I was afraid you were just going to say"—and here she pitched her voice low—"*I know it's not a goblin.*"

"Well, it isn't," came the very serious reply. High Elf Archer hid a snicker but not very well. One could only imagine how the vampire himself would have felt to hear it.

The impish imitation of his own voice was lost on Goblin Slayer but not the change in the party's mood. He could tell that even as everyone remained vigilant, they were also relaxed and loose.

I'm grateful for that.

Normally—yes, it was becoming normal, he discovered—normally, it would not have been like this. The one who was sensitive to how everyone was feeling, who passed out food and water, who performed first aid, thought things through, and kept the conversation flowing was the cleric.

Each of them made up a bit of the slack, so the party was able to function as normal.

I couldn't have done this.

If, in her absence, the unity of the party had declined, he would not have known what to do.

Rather than ponder the imponderable, Goblin Slayer turned his attention to the problem at hand—and a vampire was a substantial problem indeed.

"How many spells do you have left?"

"One or two, I'd say," Dwarf Shaman answered.

Lizard Priest volunteered that it was the same for him, his long head shaking from side to side. "I dropped my fangs. I might be able to conjure a single Dragontooth Warrior at best."

"What we need is some numbers," High Elf Archer murmured. She patted her quiver, stocked with ragged arrows, and shrugged. "If we could have scattered some more, he might have stopped again."

"But we don't know why. And if we did, we couldn't trust it," Goblin Slayer said.

"That's true," High Elf Archer said honestly. She hadn't been that serious about the remark. Arrows were her domain, and her role was as a ranger. She didn't have much to contribute to strategy meetings like this one.

Goblin Slayer had an intuition that she must, then, have had some reason for speaking up now. Before he could say anything, though, she waved it away. "It's okay. I'm doing all right. They're goblin arrows, but at least I can shoot with them."

"Good enough. Perhaps some fire powder," Goblin Slayer mused. "You said it was weak to sunlight, after all."

"You're thinkin' of bustin' through the ceiling," said Dwarf Shaman, catching on quickly. He ignored High Elf Archer's scowl and looked up. The ceiling of the passageway was right above them, but that of the large room was much higher, so far above their heads that it was cloaked in darkness. He had, indeed, spent much time and gone a great distance digging with Tunnel.

Speaking with the experience of a dwarf, the intuition of a people as comfortable under the ground as above it, he said, "I couldn't guarantee there's open sky above this temple—and I'm not sure I could get there with what I've got left."

"I see," intoned Goblin Slayer. Perhaps only a dark elf could have challenged a dwarf when it came to opinions about matters subterranean. Goblin Slayer, for his part, trusted Dwarf Shaman's judgment and didn't ask any questions.

Instead, he said, "Perhaps we could burn the creature."

"*Burn* him," High Elf Archer repeated.

"The undead oughtta catch just fine," said Dwarf Shaman. "They are *dead*, after all."

"Meaning…that thing is a corpse?" Goblin Slayer asked. There was a flicker of inspiration, the light of the God of Knowledge, in his mind. "So it has no life."

"S'pose yeh could say that, sure," said Dwarf Shaman, stroking his beard thoughtfully. Yes, it was reasonable. No one would claim that thing was alive. "In fact, there was a Vampire Lord appeared in the capital ten-odd years ago, and they actually called it the No-Life King."

In that case.

From behind his visor, Goblin Slayer looked around at his friends. His friends. He still wasn't used to thinking of them like that.

It was a little bit disappointing that their priestess wasn't here. But at the same time, it was a good thing. She was adventuring in the capital at that moment. A wonderful adventurer, far more than he could ever hope to be. He had dragged everyone else off on his own adventure, a fact Goblin Slayer found disquieting.

But if that's the case...

"I have a plan," he said. "Let's do it."

...then I have to win.

§

"Please, stand back!"

Priestess reacted immediately; she moved with precision. A brilliant display if there ever was one.

She worked her sounding staff, which jangled with every move; she leaned out from the royal box and thrust it forward.

"O Earth Mother, abounding in mercy, by the power of the land grant safety to we who are weak!"

At that instant, the winged monster that had come diving at her was pushed backward by an invisible force field and tumbled through space.

"GAAAARGO?!"

"GARGOO!!?"

One, then two of them. Priestess could feel the shock each time they slammed into Protection's field, but she held firm.

She didn't have to feel the hairs on the back of her neck stand up to know that the black dots filling the blue sky were monsters, because the experience still lived within her—the experience of the battle that had engulfed her at the fortress.

Bodies like stone. Claws, fangs, and wings. Those are...

"M-monsters...?!" Cow Girl said, terrified. "Are those demons?!"

"No!" Priestess called back. "They're gargoyles!"

It was the first time she'd seen them outside of the Monster Manual. However, even she, who had barely been on any proper adventures, was able to remain calmer than Cow Girl.

Fortunate were those who had never experienced monsters invading their home!

"GGOOYYYYLEE?!?!"

Another of the creatures smashed against the Protection barrier, and Priestess felt her hands tingle.

It's all right.

She could take it. She could still hold. There was no problem for her, she figured. But...

Chaos was already spreading among the spectators, the screams of the crowd mingling with the roars of the monsters. She saw how alert her bodyguards were and assumed the security around the audience was hopping to it as well. After all, monsters didn't just come from the sky. What if they were among you? Behind you? What would you do?

"Wh—?" came Guild Girl's tight voice. "What do we do?!"

Hers was not the cry of someone in a panic but the emphatic question of someone resolved to do something.

Priestess started calculating in her head, thinking fast. The breath came in through her delicate lips, then went out again.

"A plan—I have a plan!" she shouted so that they could hear behind her; for she had no time to turn around as another gargoyle threw itself against her barrier. "Get to the door! Hold it shut!"

"Y-yeah, okay...!" Cow Girl said, brought back to her right mind by Priestess's orders.

The royal box was, well, literally a sort of box—and it had a door for getting in and out. Rather than rushing out into the hallway in an attempt to escape, it might be better to stay in here and wait for rescue. Not, of course, that Cow Girl had thought that far ahead. It was simply that Priestess had given her instructions, and Cow Girl wasn't the kind to dawdle.

"Um, uh... A chair! We need a chair over here!" she said. "Grab that one!"

"I'm on it! Let's push together!" Guild Girl replied.

"One, two—!"

Cow Girl, like Priestess, had no time to look back, but still she and Guild Girl were able to build a crude line of defense.

King's Sister had used a miracle to put up some kind of wall, and her ladies-in-waiting were working to set up defenses—that was how it looked from the outside.

The soldiers, who had felt the entire scene growing more unreal by the second since the moment the gargoyles attacked, finally jumped into action.

"Sorry we're late! Let us help!"

"Thanks, we could use it!" Guild Girl said.

Whether you were trained or not, responding immediately was a difficult thing to do. Even adventurers, whose daily lives involved putting themselves in danger of life and limb, could sometimes be taken by surprise.

"We've got this side held down!" one of the soldiers cried.

"Thank you!"

Priestess exhaled as another gargoyle slammed downward.

Cow Girl had been in the middle of a goblin assault before—and prior to that, there had been the attack on the farm. Above all, she knew that Priestess was a strong young woman. So it would be all right. It had to be. She took comfort in that...

I don't have any plan! Priestess thought, trying to think as fast as she was able. A single bead of sweat traced a line down her forehead, then veered onto her cheek.

"Your Highness, this is dangerous! Please, you must get to safety!" a soldier yelled.

"No—"

No?

Priestess was quick to shake her head at the soldier, but suddenly she stopped. She almost put her finger to her lips, her characteristic habit, but instead she gripped the staff even harder to subdue the impulse.

If *he* was here, what would he do? At a moment like this? Was there anything in her pocket?

That's it... I see it.

Her hand was not in her pocket. It couldn't be. Both of her delicate, unreliable hands were desperately gripping her staff—she had no others.

There was a sharp sound of inhalation as Priestess took in as much air as her petite chest would hold and focused all her spirit and attention on the heavens above.

"O Earth Mother, abounding in mercy, grant your sacred light to we who are lost in darkness!" she cried.

"GGAAAAAAARRG?!?!!!!?!?"

A brilliant and holy light, blinding, filled the royal box and spilled over into the coliseum. The closest gargoyle hid its face and screamed, tumbling as it returned to a lump of stone.

It dropped, well, like a rock, slamming into the seats below and shattering—but there was a silver lining to that.

The sudden burst of holy light had pierced the chaos below, drawing every eye in the crowd. The gazes of those in the spectator seating were pulled away from their running and their disorderly flight and toward the royal box.

Who was that? Was that the princess? No one had heard of her being granted any miracles...

The murmuring started quietly; after a beat, it was swallowed up.

"As a priestess of the Earth Mother, I have a request!" Priestess said—loudly, clearly, confidently to the people below. "Any and all adventurers who are here now, lend me your aid!"

That was all she said—but the effect was dramatic. The adventurers, who had each been facing the gargoyles on their own, isolated, looked at one another.

They'd only come here to see the show. If some sparks were going to land on them, they would brush them away—it was no more than that. But this was different. They had been asked personally. By the princess of the entire nation. She had *requested* them to help deal with the monsters. And in that case, then this...

This is an adventure and nothing but!

"All right! Let's start with the big one!"

"Front rowers, over here! Protect the spell casters and clerics!"

"I've got magic! And miracles—well, just Trade God ones, but still!"

"If you've got Reverse, it'd sure come in handy!"

Parties started calling to one another, individual adventurers began teaming up, and people who had never met each other before began working together.

"Yes!" said Priestess, who had seen them all when she was casting

Holy Light. She smiled. Then she said, "Everyone else, stay calm and evacuate in an orderly fashion! The guards will help you!"

Orders were given, instructions flew. People started trusting themselves to the soldiers, who guided them out of confusion and into safety. The guards, who had fallen into panic when the monsters attacked, began to regain their composure and coherence. Yes, the situation was dangerous—but it wasn't fatal.

"Fantastic, fantastic work...," said Guild Girl with a sigh of relief and a voice full of admiration.

Cow Girl goggled; she could only find one word to describe what she had seen: *"Amazing...!"*

"Hee-hee..." Priestess smiled with just a hint of shyness, but then she tensed her cheeks again, forcing the smile away. "It's only because Goblin Slayer—and everyone else—has taught me so much!"

That's right... If you have no hands left, you just have to borrow some!

§

"Yikes... Yikes!"

That was all well and good—but not everyone was capable of immediately leaping to such distinguished action.

The black-haired girl felt the huge lump of stone graze her as it went over her head: She ducked and rolled to avoid it. It was a very close call. If she'd been wearing a hat, it might not have survived. After a second of thought, she pushed up her protective headband. She had decided to act, and this would be the best defense. Yes, this was best.

She scuttled amid the spectator seats, then gave a swing of a sword that was almost longer than she was tall.

"Hiii...yah!"

The blade sliced through the air, *wumph, wumph.* Of course, it couldn't reach the monster that floated above. The red creature arced out of the way, then came diving through the air again.

"AAAARREEMMEEEERRRRR!!!!!"

"Eeek!"

The girl with the name of the primal whirlpool rolled again, evading the deadly blow from above. She wove amid the seats once more, racing to find a different position. The monster's movements were irregular, highly unpredictable. So she stopped and observed, watching how it moved, evading when it attacked.

Move, wait, attack, dodge. That was her entire focus as she carried on the fight. She didn't have any brilliant ideas. She had simply decided to do all she could, as best she could.

"Yah! Hiyah! ...Ack! Whaaa—?!"

If she could draw even one enemy to herself, it would help the others. That was the only thought in her head—and she wasn't wrong.

The rhea fencer's blade sang out, followed by a vermilion lance that prized justice, and the half-dragon girl who planned to slay a dragon howled.

Some of the adventurers here were known; others were not. All had come from each of the four corners to be at this coliseum. And one of the monsters who would have moved to accost those adventurers didn't, because he was pinned down by this girl with the name of a storm.

The battle spreading among the spectator seats was a brutal affair, but the people held the advantage.

As for the girl, she could hardly be said to have distinguished herself. She was pathetic, even silly, but she was desperate.

"Why...you...!"

She bled from a scrape, but in her eyes and in the magic wand at her chest, there was an unmistakable spark.

This was her adventure. And if that was true, then...

"*Magna...nodos...facio!* Form, magical binding!"

...the heavenly players would certainly not leave her side.

Words of binding rumbled from somewhere, and with a crack, the monster's wings were tied up.

The girl made a sound that wasn't quite a "what?!" and wasn't quite an "oh!" She looked up and saw two adventurers.

"It's paralyzed—do it!" shouted a young woman who looked to be a wizard. At that moment, the black-haired girl thought she saw a colorful breeze slip past her.

This breeze was also in the shape of a young woman, and there came a terrible grating noise. Before the black-haired girl could

register that it was the sound of feet cracking the stone beneath them,
there was a shout:

"Diiiie!"

The cry was as sharp as any sword, and along with it, a long leg
lashed out, slamming against the monster's wings. They crumbled
into dust, and the red creature succumbed to gravity.

It was, however, still dangerous as it continued to struggle despite
half of its body having been reduced to rubble.

"Oops! Ah!" The girl hefted a sword that looked very heavy, shouted
"Yaah!" and whacked it against the creature. The huge weapon, polished with care every day, made a terrific racket as it slammed into the
creature's head, pulverizing it.

Even then, the girl wasn't sure the monster was dead. She sucked
in desperate breaths. Her hands were shaking, she stood frozen as if
paralyzed, and sweat poured down her forehead. She wiped it away
vigorously with her arm.

"Excellent work." The woman's partner, the mage, lazily waved
a hand. Only then did the black-haired girl realize the wizard was
standing in front of her.

"Oh! Um… Um!" She looked up at the other woman, and one simple word passed through her mind: *beauty*. She thought she had understood the word before, but now she realized she had known nothing.
The person in front of her wore a man's outfit, and as becoming as it
looked on her, she was without question a woman and a beautiful one.

She's wonderful…

The thought didn't cause the girl to forget the first thing she needed
to say. "Thank you…very much!" She bowed deeply, the pack on her
back shifting and rattling as she did so. She blushed furiously at it, but
the other woman surprised her.

"You've nothing to be ashamed of," she said and got down on one
knee so that she was eye to eye with the smaller, black-haired girl.
Only then did the girl realize that the other woman had just *one* eye. It
was sharp and perceptive—but also had a kind warmth. *Like the person
from the dungeoneering contest*, she thought. "You survive, you take a step
forward. One step at a time. Just keep moving."

Yeah… That I can do.

"That's…sort of my specialty."

"Very good!" The woman grinned, and her gorgeous, clear eye gazed hard at the girl, remembering her.

Seeing such a lovely older woman from this proximity naturally caused the girl to feel a bit out of sorts.

Could I…be like her?

Could she become so beautiful, so wonderful? It was hard for her to imagine.

"Uh, um…"

"Oh, pardon me." The woman smiled that luscious smile again, then brushed away the hair that hid her eye. "You just reminded me of someone I know."

"Someone you know…?"

"Mm."

Not that *he* was here. Most likely—

"That boy is off on a goblin hunt somewhere."

Even though he was too old for such things.

§

Wizard Boy had a thought: It was good that that man wasn't here.

"I knew we couldn't leave things to that king of ours. He invited this trouble," the knight grumbled, but Wizard Boy ignored him and looked around the tournament grounds, his hand on the thing he kept at his hip.

A flock of monsters—gargoyles—was attacking the spectator seating and the royal box. He'd just seen someone smash one of them. Pretty good work.

That one was kind of reddish colored. Think it was some sort of fire demon…?

It was probably quite serious stuff, then—but this wasn't the time to be ruminating. The bulk of Wizard Boy's attention was turned toward the girl, who stood on the field of combat, and on the gargoyle above her. The way it circled made the boy think of a vulture or a buzzard.

Not that I've ever seen either of those.

He didn't know if they really circled over dead bodies. Maybe he would find out one day.

If vultures didn't let their prey escape, well, neither did this gargoyle. It had both the rhea girl and the knight pinned.

Just one thing to do, then.

For the second time, he was glad that guy wasn't here. He wouldn't have admitted under torture who it was who had instilled in him the habit of always picking up things to throw.

In Wizard Boy's hand was a boomerang.

His mentor had given him grief about it: It was hellish magic, forbidden magic, a spell from a foreign land.

So what? Who gives a shit?!

The boy took one step forward, then two, gaining momentum, and then he let the thing fly.

"GARRRGG!!"

However good humans might be at throwing things, though, they were never going to get a hit 100 percent of the time. The boy didn't know whether gargoyles felt emotions, but when it juked out of the way of his boomerang, he would have sworn it was laughing at him.

But the boy was laughing, too.

"*Iacta!* Toss!" he shouted.

His entire body glowed a faint green with magical energy. The object of the word of true power that he wove from his mouth was not the boomerang but the blowing breeze.

What wizard worthy of the name didn't know the true name of at least a passing wind?

The boomerang's trajectory took an impossible turn, veering around. "GOYYYYYYY?!!!?!!?"

In the grip of the wind, the boomerang did exactly what the boy wanted, cutting through the air and slamming against the monster's wings, which vaporized with the impact.

Whatever magic one might use to cause stone wings to beat, when deprived of those wings, there could be only one result: a fall—and then death.

The drop from that height was more than enough to smash stone to pieces. The boomerang passed over the pile of debris and returned safely to the boy's hand. A magic/flying-stick combo, Wizard Boy's very own new battle tactic: the telekinetic boomerang.

He didn't have time to admire its effectiveness in battle, however. He was too busy shouting at the top of his lungs: "Finish hiiiiim!" His voice echoed across the coliseum. "Send his ass flying!"

No doubt the knight did not grasp what he meant. He probably thought the young mage was exhorting them to finish off the monster.

"I certainly will," the knight replied. "Simply let me handle this, and all will be well. From the very start, you should have—"

He didn't get to finish. Why would anyone have listened to him all the way through?

The rhea girl bellowed:

"Eyes on *me*!"

She threw aside her ruined helmet and tore off the shoulder girdle that was dangling from her chest armor.

"We're not finished yet! You can't just decide this is over!"

"____?"

The knight appeared perplexed: This was another pronouncement he didn't understand. He stood dumbfounded, and then his muffled voice could be heard from under his own headgear:

"What are you talking about?"

"My—*our*—battle with you! I don't care about anything else! And I mean *anything*!" She gestured around with her arms, her whole tiny body bouncing as she shouted. "This is the entire world!"

This was everything. They were going to settle this. Win or lose: That was everything there was.

Pierced by the gleam in the girl's eyes, the knight took one unsteady step backward. "You wish to continue our contest…?"

"Damn right I do!"

"But…" His voice wavered, troubled and confused. He held up the shattered remains of his lance. "I have no lance."

"You have your sword!"

She was not going to let him get away. She was not going to let him find an excuse.

Rhea Fighter drew her sword, the one her grandfather had given her. The nameless but beautiful blade he claimed to have found in a dungeon under the mountain.

The greatest under heaven? The strongest in the world? She couldn't be those things. But she could try. And she wouldn't let anyone laugh at her for it.

He had. This paladin had pointed and laughed. Told her she shouldn't even bother.

You wanted this fight? You've got it.

"Come at me!" she howled. "I'm gonna *rock you!*"

§

Curse these adventurers. As pleasant as plague rats.

Even as the vampire pursued the enemies, who had fled into one of the holes of his abode, he had time to reflect. To a servant of the No-Life King, the ruler of the night who had occupied the capital, adventurers were as dust underfoot.

Yet in spite of that, they had stopped the Demon Lord and his minions from spreading the Death around the four corners.

That affront was difficult to ignore.

If these bandits were going to come sneaking around his domain, he would have to punish them properly.

"Come out, come out, little adventurers…" The vampire crossed his arms as if he had all the time in the world. He shoved aside goblin corpses as he went. In his voice, there was the slightest hint of haughty magnanimity and something that sounded almost like compassion— but wasn't quite. "If you'll surrender like good boys and girls, I might even offer you eternal life."

Eternal life as my slaves!

Not as servants of the night, no—the thought didn't even cross his mind. One of the intruders had been an elf woman. If she was still a virgin, then there was every chance she might become a banshee, and he couldn't have that.

Instead, I'll enjoy sucking her blood for the rest of the eons.

This vampire was not so bored as to cultivate any buds of rebellion.

There were plenty of ways in the world to enjoy an unending life without risking such danger.

If there was anything that dissatisfied him about being a servant of the night, it was that there was no changing of the guard. Elders of dizzying age continued to hold sway—if you wanted to move up in the world, you had to get rid of them physically.

Machiavellian masquerades, then, were the order of the day...

But what of it? It lasts but a moment.

Now that he was a servant of *that* god, it would be only a matter of time until he possessed more than enough power to rid himself of that lot. And to a vampire, time was always an ally...

"I warn you, if you're hoping for rescue, you hope in vain!" That, the vampire assumed, was why they weren't moving. He even spared a chuckle. "The capital will be in shambles by now. Wait as long as you like, they will never—"

"Don't be stupid."

The voice was casual, almost mechanical, like a wind blowing deep underground. The vampire should never have been able to hear it, yet somehow it reached his ears.

With his literally monstrous vision, he spotted his prey leaping out of the passageway faster than the speed of sound. "There are adventurers in the capital," said the adventurer buried in the grimy armor, his voice almost a growl. "Adventurers far greater than I."

"Clean water, dirty water, mixed together like cloudy weather, nothing can be seen through!"

At that same moment, a rotund little dwarf scattered the contents of a wine jug at his hip while singing a silly little song. The droplets *fssh*ed and *fzz*ed and became a clinging mist that filled the shrine.

Absurdity!

Nonetheless, the vampire's smile remained like a crimson tear in his face. No doubt the dwarf had used Invisible or some other trick like that. Yes, that might have worked on the likes of goblins. But him?

They have no idea why *vampires can see in the dark, do they?*

The world vampires saw was not one bathed in light. Vampires saw heat. They saw *life.* Their senses were spiritual in nature; they didn't depend upon their physical eyes.

Even if those droplets were magical, it was an affront that the adventurers had imagined they would be of any use.

Ah, what fools these mortals be...

Now the vampire knew victory was within his grasp, and he had no time to hiss and spit about a childish prank like this.

"Enough of this!"

He swept away the arrows that came flying at him through the mist, then bounded forward. He could tell there were flickering flames racing at him like lightning through the mists of Invisible from left and right. It must be that impertinent creature who spoke to him a moment ago. That must be their leader. Yes, kill him first.

The scruffy armor emerged from the mist. The vampire's sword was raised and ready.

He would cleave him apart with a single stroke. Crush his head like an overripe melon and trample on his corpse.

"Now you die!" the vampire bellowed and reduced his opponent to dust. His opponent, who was only a pile of white bones. "Wha—?!"

The vampire looked in every direction: Much against his will, he found his eyes forced to follow the pieces as they scattered.

He didn't know what had happened. He was sure that an instant ago, he had been fighting their leader, the one they referred to as Goblin Slayer or some such thing. And now, in his place, there were only bones.

A dragon's skull. A dragon soldier. Fine—but where had it come from? Had it taken the adventurer's place? When had they made the switch?

No! That isn't what happened...

He spotted the small pouch the man was holding. Its mouth was open, and the dragon soldier was emerging from it...

"A bag for holding?!" the vampire yelled. In temporal terms, he was frozen for less than a second. "So I missed a single move—so what?!"

"One move is all I need." The steel helmet was close now, with that darkness behind its visor. That growling voice. "I'm told you're a corpse—is that right?"

The next second, the vampire felt the bag come down on his head.

"Whaaaaaa—?!"

He didn't even have time to finish his howl before the bag slipped over him, swallowing him up. A world of blackness, even for this servant of the night who could see in the dark. No sound, no air. He could scratch and scrabble, but it gained him nothing. As he watched, his arms, his torso, his legs were all consumed by the bag.

"In that case, I can put you away," came a voice from behind and above, like a sentence of death. "Because you are just a *thing*."

"No! Undone by the machinations of a mere munchkin…!"

The vampire rained curses on the heads of his enemies, but they never made it out of the bag. Soon he was lost to the endless void.

"Farewell," came the voice, and then with merciful quickness, all light vanished.

§

The fight ended as abruptly as it had begun. No sooner was the vampire in the bag than the zombies, their master no longer on the same plane as them, collapsed. All that remained was dust, a pile of ashes. And the adventurers—living and breathing.

They remained vigilant, weapons and catalysts at the ready, keeping a close watch all around. After all, the vampire hadn't been destroyed. He might have some hidden trick up his sleeve yet. He might even be able to tear open the bag and escape.

The aching silence was finally broken by a single disinterested sentence. "That was excellent work."

Goblin Slayer gingerly tied the bag shut, then picked up the skull by his feet: the Dragontooth Warrior, its duty fulfilled. How many times had these nonspeaking servants saved him and his party?

Is there some way to reward them?

He never seemed to be able to find an answer to that question—no matter of what or whom he was asking it. For the only thing he was capable of doing was killing goblins.

"…Are we alive? We *are* alive, aren't we?" High Elf Archer asked now that Goblin Slayer had cut the thread of tension. She threw herself down spread-eagled on the ash-covered floor, grinning like a child tired from playing too much. That even so, she appeared unutterably elegant—well, this was why the bards loved to sing of the elves. "Gods above, I'm exhausted! And we didn't even get to see the tournament…!"

"They tell me she's an elf princess. Not sure I believe it, though," Dwarf Shaman grumbled—but then he laughed. Yes, this princess of the elves was confident that the tournament had in fact been held in the capital; she didn't doubt it. Maybe there had been a little trouble— a little adventure—but that kind of trouble meant business for them.

There were adventurers there. Including a friend of theirs—the priestess. How much of a problem could there be?

Guess she and I are probably on the same page, thinkin' that.

"Well, best hope that's the end of it. I'm fresh outta spells," Dwarf Shaman said.

"And I as well," added Lizard Priest. It had taken everything he had to go toe-to-toe with the vampire. He sat down heavily on the floor; if left to his own devices, he looked like he might just curl up right there. His fingers played across the staff of the Earth Mother, which he held in his hands, and he shook his long head gently. "In the end, we never did figure out why that monster stopped whenever he saw bones."

"I didn't expect to," said Goblin Slayer, tossing the bones to Lizard Priest. "We were lucky."

"Indeed, even so."

"It was my suggestion! Make sure you give me the credit!" High Elf Archer cut in.

"Naturally," said Goblin Slayer, his helmet moving up and down. "I wouldn't have thought of it."

"Somehow that doesn't feel much like a compliment…" High Elf Archer's head drooped, but from the way her ears flicked, she seemed to be in a good mood.

If they didn't have enough dragon fangs, why not get more from a Dragontooth Warrior? They might not serve as catalysts, but a bone was a bone. It might be enough for a distraction.

It had been High Elf Archer's idea, if not her greatest pleasure.

A bag for holding…

The bag, tied shut, didn't so much as twitch. Of course it didn't: There was nothing living within it.

They could put the Dragontooth Warrior inside and then unleash it in front of the enemy. It would serve as their shield; all it had to do was distract the opponent when he destroyed it. Even if it didn't succeed at that, it would absorb his first blow.

All they needed was a single action to enable them to slip the bag over the vampire.

"Let this be a lesson to you, Orcbolg: You could do with having a few magic items on hand."

"That's more than I need for dealing with goblins."

Ugh!

He wasn't wrong—but High Elf Archer nonetheless gave a dramatic click of her tongue and made an exceptionally distressed face. This was nothing new with him—he had always been this way.

He just took out a vampire without using any explosions, fire, or floods...

For Orcbolg, that was pretty good.

"Tell me, Beard-cutter," Dwarf Shaman began, sipping the very last of his fire wine. "What was your plan if you couldn't get the vampire in the bag—or if he got back out?"

"I didn't have any plan to speak of," Goblin Slayer said succinctly. "I assumed I would put my remaining fire powder in the bag and light it."

High Elf Archer stared at the ceiling, speechless.

§

We need hardly speak of what became of the vampire after that. Perhaps he was dumped out of the bag into a bright patch of sunlight, or perhaps a torch was tossed in the bag with him. Hell, maybe it was both.

The point is, the vampire himself never knew in what way he was reduced to ashes.

§

"Gyyyaaaaahhhhh!"

"Hrngh?!"

The primal scream was accompanied by a blow as fast and as hard as lightning. Like lightning, it didn't give the knight so much as a second to say anything.

In fact, the rhea girl had never been of a mind to give that bastard a chance to open his mouth.

Instead, the coliseum echoed with a cry more monstrous than that of any of the gargoyles.

She flew in—yes, she seemed to move as if she had wings—to deliver the blow faster than the eye could see.

In the space of a breath, that blow was followed by ten more, twenty, thirty.

"This isn't...! This is brutality... You might as well be wielding a club...! This isn't swordsmanship!"

It was to the knight's credit that he was able to bring his weapon up at all. Even if it couldn't do much more than take the blow, it prevented the stroke from landing on his head.

"Gyyyaaaaahhhhh!"

She's insane...! Beneath his helmet, the blood had drained from the knight's face, and he was scowling hard. The opponent pressing in on him—a rhea girl so small he had to look down to see her—seemed far larger than she was. The knight took two steps back, then three, as if he was facing a giant, not a rhea. *She's only charging forward! I can deal with that!*

"Hrrah!" He swung his blade down hard—but the rhea girl wasn't there.

He heard a *zhwf* as her bare feet scuttled across the sand; the speed with which she put herself behind him was unreal. This was footwork that could only be achieved with the stubborn feet of a rhea. The girl had learned that from her grandfather, a person of few words but much knowledge.

He had been an adventurer himself. He'd delved the dungeon depths beneath the mountain, and his own heel had been pierced. She didn't know if it had been from a trap or if it was the doing of a monster. She knew only that it had put an end to his career in swordsmanship.

"What we practice, 'tain't a strong blade. 'Tis a fast one."

That was what he had told her as he had her strike a tree as fast as she could, morning and night.

"To make a fast blade work, you have to put your energy into every stroke. Otherwise your sword is no better than a kitchen knife."

She shouted and beat the tree until she was out of breath. She hit the tree as hard as she could. Never letting her stance falter, stroke after stroke.

"A blade needs proper energy—but never put your heart into it. For the sword has no heart."

He said it was so that she could practice anywhere, anytime—and everywhere, all the time. Even if the people around her mocked her, laughed at her, said there was no way she could do it.

"Swing the sword with your heart, and in time, without even trying, you'll be like lightning."

Her grandfather died. There was a plague, and then he was gone. She couldn't believe how sudden it was.

She heard people talk: *"Now that girl will stop with her foolishness. She'll settle down and get married."* They didn't ask what she wanted—they just tried to make things the way *they* wanted.

It made her sick. She ignored them. That was why she was here now. That was how she had gotten here.

"Gggyyaaahhh!"

"Hrk?! What in blazes does she thinks she's—? I've never seen such absurd swordsmanship!"

She didn't care. She wasn't listening. At that point, the girl wasn't even thinking anymore.

There was only one thing in her head—or perhaps two.

Swing the sword. Move forward. Swing the sword. Move forward. Swing the sword. Move forward.

You've got to strike! someone cried in her mind. It was the little girl mocked and ridiculed by all and sundry.

You've got to strike. For that little girl.

You've got to strike. For your grandfather.

You've got to strike. For the slightly deranged mentor whose ideas she could never quite follow.

You've got to strike. For the older girl on the farm. For the people of that decent frontier town. For her friends.

You've got to strike. For him, the one who had brought her this far.

"Gyyyyaaahhheeee!"

"Hrn...?! She—! What?! But how?!"

Her sword blazed with a flare, the aura of the gods. The thoughts and feelings of the people in the Four-Cornered World, their very wills, now imbued her blade through the bonds they shared.

It was a light that would be incomprehensible to those who chose the path of Chaos, who sought to bend the world to their will. Therefore— yes, that was why, as an explosion like the sun lit the coliseum from somewhere far overhead...

"H-hrgh?!"

"Yaaaaaaahhhh!"

The paladin stumbled backward, his eyes seared by the light, and the girl leaped forward with the light at her back.

It was one-eighth of one breath. No, one-tenth of even that. Another tenth. Then another. Then another. In fact, the blade was like lightning as it crossed the battlefield.

"?!?!?!"

The paladin cried out a wordless scream. He raised his sword to defend, and it shattered in his hand—truly, a bequest of good fortune. The attacking blade slammed into his shoulder, smashing the joint clear through his armor. His left arm fell limp, and then so did the paladin, tumbling to the ground.

"Ahhh... A— Arrgh! The pain...!"

Finally, the contest was settled. The rhea girl lowered her sword and replaced it in its scabbard with a trembling hand. She had done it—somehow.

Her body felt as heavy as lead; sweat poured off her in a waterfall. She thought she could see it pooling at her feet.

She fought the urge to fall to her knees. She sucked in oxygen, her chest heaving up and down.

She felt faint, and there was a ringing in her ears; she couldn't hear anything. Couldn't hear? No...

*　　*　　*

"_____!!"

It was her name.

The spectator stands were in a terrible state, spattered with blood, riddled with monster corpses. Seats were broken and crushed. Yet in spite of it all, the people were cheering. They were shouting her name.

The adventurers who had finished their fight, the soldiers, the returned spectators. All of them were cheering for her.

"_____…!"

For the first time, the girl could only stand dumbly. She couldn't believe it. Was this really happening? She'd never even dreamed about this. It seemed impossible.

She looked around, her eyes welling up with tears, and then finally she shuffled forward. Her first step was unsteady, her second more of a stumble, but with the third, she flung herself onward, hurtling headlong.

We hardly need say where she was going.

She let the momentum carry her straight to the red-haired boy and caught him up in a hug.

"We are the champions, my friend!"

"Whoa! Ack…!"

Unable to slow her down, the boy toppled on the ground. He noticed the girl's warmth, her softness, her smell. He felt agitation. Excitement. Joy. Embarrassment. It was like he was feeling every possible emotion at once.

Was that her who was crying, or was it him? He didn't even know. They hugged each other and rubbed their eyes—but the boy still managed to find time for a good rebuke.

"You…you dummy! What do you mean, champions?!"

"Well, aren't we?!"

She was a mess of tears and snot and weeping—and yet (the thought flashed through his mind) she was still beautiful.

He tried to pretend he hadn't had the thought by saying, "It's not the finals yet!" And then he poured all his many emotions into mussing her hair. She shrieked, but soon she was laughing, laughter that echoed all around the coliseum.

To close this chapter, however, it seems appropriate to quote from one of the heroic sagas.

On that day, the coliseum echoed endlessly with cheers for a rhea swordmaster.

YOUR EYES ONLY

Adventurers. What a load of trash, thought the man as he worked his way back down the fighters' corridor of the coliseum. Behind him, the stadium rang with cheers.

Somewhere in the melee, his servant had gone, his horse had vanished; he couldn't even get his armor off. His battered shoulder felt unresponsive and hot; agony ran through it with every breath. His left arm still hung limply.

It was plain to see that this was someone who had been defeated and defeated utterly. And yet…

What is the king thinking, allowing lawless ruffians like those to run free?

The man's thoughts were not those of someone who was gracious in defeat; they were filled with contempt and hatred.

Perhaps we should not be surprised.

Contests that focused on martial strength alone were the height of barbarity. Discrimination against the weak in its purest form! The man trembled to think what would happen if such savages were set loose in every land.

Other countries were more enlightened than his own, more civilized. This nation couldn't be left in its backward ways. From what he heard, there were no adventurers on the plains to the east, nor in the country of deserts, nor in the frozen lands to the north. His own home should establish such a progressive system. Everything he did was to that end.

And yet…!

And yet they had put on this tournament, an orgy of dissipation and debauchery. Moreover, the king's younger sister, whom he had thought might be the cornerstone of a brighter future, had proven obstinate in her benighted ignorance.

And the way she had wielded a weapon—an actual weapon!—against the forces of Chaos; well, what could be further removed from peace? Such behavior would never lead to a better, stronger world.

I must continue. I must let the poor and the ignorant know of my mission.

The common people were thoughtless and easily deceived. It was so very difficult to convince them of truth and justice. Behind its facade, the world roiled with conspiracies and plots, and it was incumbent upon him to share what he knew, to make right the people's understanding.

First and foremost—at the very least—that king had to be deposed…

"Hrm…?"

Only then did the man register that something was strange.

It's silent.

There was no one else in the passageway; he was all alone. Standing there all by himself.

That shouldn't have been possible. There were always people here, soldiers, during the tournament. Notwithstanding the monster attack—in fact, that should have meant *more* soldiers.

Why had the monsters poured out from a magical rift anyway? They could have used this passage to get in. And yet it seemed—

"You don't look like a man who's ready to accept defeat. Am I right?"

"…?!"

Only when that voice spoke did he realize someone was there. A knight who sidled out in front of him to block his way. Beside him, an attendant with silver hair followed like a shadow.

The beaten man stopped moving, and for a second, his voice grew tight. It didn't stop him from snapping, "Who the hell are you? Only authorized personnel are allowed in here!" He felt disgust well up at the way this interloper had brought along a young woman as well. "If you're any kind of a knight, you should know better than to bring an innocent young woman to a battlefield. Have some shame!"

"Hey, now. If you're helping to run this show, you ought to at least have a sense of who's involved."

"What's that mean?"

"It means I *am* authorized personnel." The knight appeared to smile. "A competitor, in fact."

Oblivious to the silver-haired lady's murderous look, the man studied this new knight—and then he remembered. Several of the knights participating in the tournament had chosen, each for reasons of their own, not to compete under their real names. Yes, and this knight had been one of them, standing alongside some young women bearing the sigil of the Trade God.

Ah yes, behold his shimmering accoutrements! Even in the darkness of the passageway, the knight's armor and shield and helmet, his gauntlet, and the sword at his hip all shone with a piercing light.

The healing blessing, the light that disperses evil, the charm of unfreezing, the primal flame, the tempestuous wind: The knight before him bristled with imposing magical items, and his name was...

"The Knight of Diamonds...!"

He was a legend in his own way, spoken of among the common people. A quiet legend, almost a fairy tale. The story had spread quickly among the townsfolk these last years—but it was only a fantasy.

The story told of a "knight of the streets," who hid his face and dealt justice to evildoers in the dark.

Surely it was only a story. But that Knight of Diamonds stood now before this man.

Stupidest name I've ever heard...

Diamonds, his ass! It was the sort of thing a child with an overactive imagination would come up with. Besides, if he really thought he was going to cut down every crooked merchant, every corrupt noble, every adherent of some dark and evil sect—what would that make him but a mass murderer?

The fact that the king allowed such a monster to run free was the utmost proof of his incompetence!

"You appoint yourself to pass judgment, and you call it justice," the man said. "In my view, you're nothing but a common killer."

The Knight of Diamonds met the man's attack with an approving grin. "You condemn me? That's your right, but you should have raised your objection *before* you approved my participation in this tournament. However, the problem we're here to deal with today is you."

"What?"

Did the knight mean to cut him down, then? The man's pallor shifted—not from fear but from mockery. Would that not be the final evidence that this Knight of Diamonds was nothing but a criminal? That he knew no shame for anything he did?

The man opened his mouth to tell the Knight of Diamonds exactly what he thought of his behavior—but he was shut up before he could speak even a single syllable.

"I sent to the water town with details of how you've acted and begged the archbishop for her judgment," the knight said. "It seems you've caused a great deal of trouble. Inconvenienced many people. She did not sound pleased."

In his hands, the Knight of Diamonds held a letter. The man had no idea of what it had been through to reach this place—how many people had died, how many adventures had been had bringing it here. Perhaps there was no point in wondering what spies had been involved in its transport; they had done their duty, and that was all.

No matter how many times his face might change, no matter how many times he might die—he was a man who loved the same wine, used the same weapons, and made the impossible possible. That great doer of deeds had never once failed in a mission—and the fruit of his labors was here now.

But such plotting, such doings in the dark were far removed from the man who stood here. Only evil people, only those steeped in darkness, would dirty their hands with such things.

"I was informed that you've acted entirely alone, without advice from or reference to either the wishes of your temple or the teachings of your religion," the knight said.

"You would believe that woman's ravings? The poor girl was broken when she was attacked by goblins!" How dare he? How dare the Knight of Diamonds try to hide behind a woman? He was the bottom of the barrel, this man. Not even worthy of being called a knight. The man's tongue was quick and sharp. "She's only a puppet of that rabble at the Temple of Law. She can't make her own decisions, and that's to their benefit!"

"You seem to enjoy finding fault with the failings of others."

"That's not what I'm talking about!" the man nearly shouted. Only then did he register the pounding of blood in his ears. He leaned forward, heedless of the pain in his left shoulder, and shouted, spittle flying from his mouth. "I'm only saying that we cannot let ourselves be trapped by retrograde ideas in which heroism consists only of achievement in battle—"

"You are, of course, right that the teachings of every deity must be constantly reexamined and renewed—but it is not your place to decide them alone."

Anyway, one heard that the justice of the Supreme God did not lie in the expiation of evil. It was in the ceaseless questioning of what *was* good and evil.

"Tell me… Tell me one thing," the man said. If, in spite of this truth, they were doing justice by expunging evil… "What god, what deity, gave you this revelation?"

There was a sound, a gentle rustling, and a breeze blew from somewhere unknown through the suffocating corridor. It brought with it a piercing chill, weaving between the knight and the lady and then the man before continuing to wherever it was going. In its wake, it left only a faint, bitter taste of ash in the air.

"Who—?"

Who the hell does this "knight" think he is?!

The man didn't even realize that his right hand was reaching for the sword at his hip; his eyes glazed with hatred. The Knight of Diamonds—his ass! This was the man who had received the golden spur? He was an outlaw!

That armor he was wearing—he'd probably stripped it off a corpse on some battlefield somewhere.

"You have no right to complain about what I do! Who died and made you king?!"

"Who indeed?" The knight—the Knight of Diamonds—appeared to laugh. "Funny. I was wondering the same thing about you."

"…What…?"

"Each time you speak, the words you wield are like a blade fashioned for that particular occasion. They lack any consistency."

Sigh. The lady-in-waiting shook her head at this, appearing exasperated. She looked at the man with eyes as cold as ice and whispered that he should just play along.

The expression, the body language—the man remembered them. In his mind, the pieces fell into place with an audible click. "I know you! You're the king's dog—his little pet!"

She was the *king's* attendant. This was all the proof he needed that the king and the Knight of Diamonds were colluding with each other. A genuine smile came over the man's face. This was absurd! Perfect! More than enough to drag the king off his throne. The man would never get another chance like this.

His hand tightened on his scabbard, but he couldn't draw yet. He was going to cut down his opponent, and he needed the right excuse.

Luckily for him, he had it. For the knight had mocked him. *And if I revile someone, hate them—does that not show that they are evil?*

"You may try to humiliate me, but it will do you no good! I *will* let the world know of your misdeeds, and you *will* face judgment!" he hollered—but there was no answer.

Instead, the Knight of Diamonds raised the visor of his helmet ever so slightly and said, "Are you so quick to forget my face?"

"?!?!"

A moment later, the man lunged at the Knight of Diamonds. He gibbered incomprehensibly, clutching his sword in his hand, taking a great swing.

He wasn't even aware that the sword he struck with was already broken in half. His eyes blazed; he bared his teeth; he reveled in the joy of destroying an opponent. It was not the face of a human being.

It was no longer a man who threw himself at the Knight of Diamonds—but a beast who had heard the whispering of the External God.

"Keerraahhhhh!" he cried.

"I want you to know, I'm not here because you opposed me at every turn," the knight said abruptly. "It's because you dragged my little sister into this."

This crazed beast was no match for the Knight of Diamonds. His vorpal blade decapitated the creature effortlessly, a single fatal stroke. The man's vision filled with the void spinning around him once, and then he bounced along the ground once, twice—and then everything went dark.

Even without its life force, the body continued to writhe on the ground; the silver-haired lady-in-waiting promptly dispatched it with her dagger. The likes of this thing deserved no more honorable death.

Once, then twice, her blade plunged into his heart. Then she got to her feet.

"...So?" There wasn't a speck of blood on her outfit; she remained the picture of a pure, faithful servant. "What will we tell them? That after he was injured in the tournament, things went downhill from there?"

"No... That would cast a pall over the girl's victory."

"What do we say, then?"

"What, you don't know?" The knight shook the blood off his blade and returned it to its scabbard with a fittingly royal motion. He looked exactly as he had when he'd faced the No-Life King here in the capital—although, in fact, much time had passed. "He had a stomach ailment of some kind, let's say, and with the conclusion of his participation in this tournament, he intends to keep to strict bed rest, his emoluments to be granted to his family."

"Sure. That's what we'll go with."

If it wasn't going to be an issue for the silver-haired attendant, she had scant further interest in it. It would be a problem for the red-haired cardinal, but she could safely ignore it.

Besides...

The man had bound himself to an evil sect, tried to disrupt the tournament—indeed, tried to perpetrate terror in the royal capital. And his method had been to attempt to curse the girl—not even because she was a member of the royal family! For the likes of him, this young woman had little compassion indeed.

Guess our hands are tied, though.

There was nothing more tiresome than politics—it had so many rules. That was what made it politics. If they just went around killing everyone they didn't like because they didn't like them…

We'd be no better than him.

"…I'm starting to think adventuring might have been easier," she muttered.

She felt the weight of the Knight of Diamonds's rough gauntlet on her head; he mussed her hair. It wouldn't help—he couldn't distract her that way.

She pouted even more fiercely than usual and said, "I'll deal with this guy. You get some distance." But all the same, she placed her hand over his and didn't push him away. "Just try not to be too serious. Please."

"How's that?"

"The demons who poured from that portal…" The young woman looked around the passageway; the touch of evil had departed from the corpse, and now the place was no more remarkable than any other hallway. "You struck them all down in one fell swoop, and you're still not satisfied?"

"Oh, how many times am I going to get a chance like this?" The knight was always this way. He chuckled calmly, looking the way he did when he wanted to go into a dragon's den. "Anyway, my opponent is just a girl dressed in green wielding an iron spear—well loved by the Trade God."

"You're not going to fight a hero with an enchanted blade?"

"Don't be silly." The knight appeared unbothered by the young woman's barb. This was what made him so much work!

"Gods above…"

The young woman smiled in spite of herself. The knight ran his fingers through her hair, and then he set off. The commotion in the coliseum was over, and the tournament would soon begin again—it needed to. If they let this cause them to shrink back and give up their plans, it would be exactly what the enemy wanted.

They could not give in to the god of death and ashes, who wished to burn everything to the ground. They could not bend to evil. That cult would take any excuse to light a flame, but that was all it was—an excuse because they wanted to burn.

A truly fair world—would that not be a world that everyone can enjoy? In which all people share laughter?

As he prepared to leave, the knight knelt down and, just once, spared a look at the man's lifeless corpse.

May the soul of this sorry man be judged fairly, as he wished.

And with that, the Knight of Diamonds walked away.

IT'S A WONDERFUL LIFE!

One: *"O Earth Mother, abounding in mercy…"*

The other: *"By your revered hand…"*

Together: *""Cleanse this land!""*

A whisper, a prayer, an incantation. The two clerics performed the rite of supplication faultlessly.

The portal, the dark magic that rent the earth, believed to lead directly to the depths of the abyss—the ring of fire that burned in the stone floor, slicing into the world with a depthless darkness. The castle was located directly over this place in no small part to seal it up.

I never even imagined! But…

A faint, gentle light surrounded them, centering upon the holy staff blessed by the Earth Mother—as well as the two clerics who stood to either side of it, mirror images of each other and yet completely different.

Of course, they were nothing like each other. And of course, it was only natural that they *were* like each other.

One was a young woman raised as an orphan on the frontier, who sought to become an adventurer and advanced step by step toward her goal.

The other was a young woman raised as the little sister of a king, and after a great fall, she rose again to advance toward her goal.

Everything about the two of them was different: what they wanted, what they had, who they were, what they'd experienced. And yet they had confronted their challenges. They had helped and been helped. And now they stood hand in hand, performing a rite as one. Even though they were still so different.

The gods of the Four-Cornered World saw it, and it was good. The Earth Mother honored them and bent her ear to their request. The light, as sweet and warm as it was powerful, held the room as if in the palm of her hand. The brightness washed over everything, and when it melted away...

"Phew..."

...what was left was only a big pit, bereft of all awfulness.

"Very good work. That's the end of it... Isn't it?" Priestess asked, putting a hand to her petite chest in relief.

"Yes! Thank you!" King's Sister said, catching her up in a hug.

"Eep!" Priestess exclaimed, stumbling, her body still delicate although by now well honed.

For reasons they couldn't fathom, the curse that had afflicted King's Sister had vanished even before the staff had arrived. After regaining all her energy in the space of a single night, her complaint was only that she had missed all the excitement at the tournament.

As for Priestess, she didn't feel that her or her party members' efforts had been in vain. Instead, she thought, *Thank goodness*, and she meant it with all her heart.

"Are you sure it was really all right, though?" Priestess asked, cocking her head in perplexity even as she continued to hug the other girl who, despite being her own age, was considerably plumper.

"Was what all right?"

The other girl looking up at her from such close range made her heart skip a beat, and she wasn't sure why. The face looked so much like her own, and yet its expressions were completely unique. She found herself smiling with the wonder of it.

"I mean, for me to take on such an important role... Twice!"

"Who else could have done it? If you go getting all concerned about it, I won't have anyone left turn to."

"Well, that's true enough..."

Performing this ritual was one thing—she was a cleric of the Earth

Mother, after all—but impersonating the king's little sister? The very idea!

It's like the story of the prince and the pauper.

Or the cutpurse girl who traded places with a princess.

The world teemed with stories of such adventures, and yet she had never imagined she might find herself in one of them!

"You're lucky… I just spent the whole time sleeping!"

"Well, the important thing is, you're okay. To think—a curse! I was shocked when I heard."

"Yeah, a human sacrifice!" King's Sister giggled. "That's twice now!" She wondered aloud if *that* was her curse. Not a funny thought—but Priestess couldn't help smiling.

"If that's *your* curse… Well, just think of how many times I've been goblin hunting!"

"True……"

King's Sister produced such a pregnant, indescribable look that Priestess shot her another puzzled glance.

"Are you sure you're all right?" Priestess asked.

King's Sister was quick to add, "I don't mean I'm not grateful, you know? I mean, for this time and last time. But this is a separate issue!"

"Ah." Priestess nodded. "Don't worry about it!"

"You mean that?"

"Yep!" That small chest puffed out—humbly but with some measure of confidence. "I do like to think I've learned a thing or two about goblin hunting, after all!"

Without a word, King's Sister put her hands to her face and turned toward the ceiling as if she were praying to the Earth Mother.

The gesture was so much *like* her friend that Priestess burst out laughing.

§

With the rite completed, Priestess returned the Earth Mother's staff to King's Sister and then left the demonic portal. It was a big national secret, so when she shut the door behind her, none of her friends were waiting for her.

The castle hallway was more opulent than any she had yet seen. Her feet sank into a thick rug, while the walls and windows were adorned with metalwork. Moreover, there were tapestries of the warriors of light who carried the four orbs and of the three generations who had delved for the dragon. The windows were as translucent as ice, and sunlight poured through them, warm, pleasant, and golden. And yet...

Why is this place so big?

It just didn't sit right with her. She'd been to various temples that were bigger than this castle hallway, and yet...

Oh! I haven't heard about the others' adventure!

It wasn't unusual for her and her friends to go on separate adventures, but of course she wanted to know how things had gone for them. And she wanted to tell them how hard she had worked.

They were probably getting ready to go by now, so maybe they were near the castle gate? Priestess, suddenly in a hurry, jogged down the massive corridor. Sure, an onlooker might chide her for such unladylike behavior, but running through a castle—

Isn't that an adventure in itself?

"...Hee-hee!"

It was an amusing little excuse, and it made her happy; her steps grew lighter with it.

Just try not to stumble, try not to fall. Imagine you're going along with a ten-foot pole.

And watch out for random encounters around any corner you might turn...

"Ah, there you are."

"Eep...?!" Priestess yelped, hurriedly straightening up and taking off her cap. There, just around the corner, was a handsome man whose looks evoked a young lion.

I never expected to run into His Majesty the King here!

Well, that was what made it a random encounter, wasn't it? The same turn of chance that could see you meet a dragon in the open field.

"Er, uh, that is, pardon me. Please excuse my unconscionable rudeness..."

"Think nothing of it." King waved a hand merrily, both accepting and dismissing Priestess's apology. "If there's anything unconscionable here, it's the trouble to which I've put you."

"N-no, sire! Not at all!"

"I'll see that a proper thanks and…a reward will be sent to the western frontier. You have my gratitude."

Priestess managed to squeak out, "Th-thank you very much, Sire…"

"Mm," said King. He nodded, and then for a long moment, he studied Priestess's face.

"……?"

Priestess, much puzzled, could hardly breathe; she felt like she had been placed under a petrification curse. Somehow she managed to both feel completely frozen and fidget awkwardly at the same time.

She was anxious, yes—but strangely, not uncomfortable.

Sometime thereafter, King closed his eyes, sighed deeply, and then asked slowly, "Do you enjoy your adventures?"

"Yes, sir!" Priestess responded without a moment's hesitation. A shy smile appeared on her face. Here, at least, was a question she could answer with confidence. "They involve a lot of difficult things, a lot of problems, a lot of pain…"

"Is that so?"

But despite it all, adventures were still fun, Priestess informed the young king. At that, he smiled and nodded.

"I remember it myself. The pleasure of advancing forward… Even if it got me in trouble sometimes."

Gripped by what seemed to be nostalgia, he rubbed the back of his neck. Priestess wasn't sure what the gesture meant. She understood, though, that it was born of a memory of adventure that this person had experienced. A recollection of some important quest that only he knew about, that no one else could imagine.

And I have them, too.

Memories of adventures like that. It had only been a few years, but she would hold them forevermore.

"…"

Did the young king know what she was thinking? He didn't say anything, but a slight smile came over his face—for a second. Then he tightened his lips, and the smile was gone as if it had never been there. In its place was an expression of seriousness that made Priestess stop and swallow hard.

Finally, King said only: "See that you remain a friend to my little sister. Please."

"Yes, sir!" Priestess replied, again without hesitation—what else could she say? "She *is* my friend, after all!"

There was not a bit of flattery in this; she wasn't simply saying what he wanted to hear.

For a moment, the king of the whole nation regarded her expression, bright as the morning sun, with a smile in his eyes.

Then, after a moment of silence in which he seemed to be searching the air for the right words, he said, "As her older brother, you have my gratitude. Thank you."

"Oh! No, I—I mean... You're welcome." Priestess scratched her cheek, then coughed discreetly. "*Ahem*, I, uh, I should be going now." Everyone was waiting for her, she added, and then she bowed to him. She put her cap back on her head and scuttled down the corridor with the gait of a little bird.

The young king of the whole nation watched her go for a silent moment, and then he turned on his heel and walked away.

The shorter a conversation between the king and an adventurer, the better.

That was the way it was, and the way it ought to be.

King knew that better than anyone.

§

"Argh! I can't believe I lost!"

"Will you give it a rest?"

Beneath a dizzyingly blue sky, a donkey loaded down with armor and equipment meandered down the road. A boy held the reins while beside him walked a rhea girl whose body language expressed her feelings even more eloquently than her words. She swung her arms furiously as she walked along, making no effort at all to hide her frustration.

The wizard boy (the rhea girl had practically talked his ear off by this point) heaved a sigh and said, "Yeah, you definitely peaked when you left that paladin flat on his ass."

"Arrrrgh… I fell! I can't *believe* I *fell* out of my *saddle!*"

This time, the girl clutched her head in her hands and curled up right there on the road home, so the boy was obliged to stop alongside her. The donkey, unbothered by its masters' strange behavior, scuffed its hooves.

In truth, the donkey had acquitted itself well. It had held its own against proper warhorses; fine work indeed. Responsibility for the defeat therefore fell squarely on its rider. Her display of ferocity had left her exhausted, and she was easily bested in the next round. To be fair, the knight who'd un-donkeyed her hadn't gone on to the finals, either, but that was cold comfort.

"…Arrrgh…" The rhea girl threw herself onto the grass by the roadside, spreading her arms.

Wizard Boy looked down at her and stated the obvious: "We're right by the road."

"It's still a square of the Four-Cornered World! I can be here if I want!" The girl flailed her bare feet.

"I haven't heard a hairsplitting like that since the Academy." That was all Wizard Boy said by way of reprobation, though. He plopped down beside her. "Guess it just means we've still got farther to go."

"Yeah…"

When she thought back, she saw what a collection of powerful warriors they had been among. What had they even been doing there?

For instance—there had been many memorable matches, but to take just one example—she'd seen a spectacular competition between a knight wearing the vestments of the Trade God and another knight in diamonds.

We shall prescind from speaking of who won…

"That was really something, wasn't it?" the rhea girl said.

"…Uh-huh."

Idle chatter passed between them as they sat there with the grass and the breeze around them and the sky over their heads.

There was frustration, yes. There was disappointment. But not a single regret.

There are loftier heights to reach. We can keep moving forward.

That's all it meant.

Heck, this was their first time in a competition like this one, and look how well they'd done. What was there to be depressed about in that? It would be simple arrogance to be dissatisfied just because you didn't win your first tournament. They could hold their heads up high with the result they had reached. The result they had earned.

After a moment, Wizard Boy stood up, crying, "Okay!"

"Yikes!" exclaimed the rhea girl, who was still lying on the ground. She sat up (using only her toned abdominal muscles) and looked at him. "You sure sound excited."

"'Course I am! Time is unlimited and limited. We can't just sit around here!"

"I dunno. I think it's important to slow down and enjoy the journey sometimes. Hup!" The girl got to her feet, laughing, and brushed the grass off her behind. "So where do we go next?"

"Dunno yet," the boy said with a grin. "But you don't really want to go straight back to the old guy, do you?"

"If you've got a good idea for a detour, I'm all ears." The rhea girl grinned like a kid with a mischievous plan.

They didn't know where they would go exactly. But they knew where they were headed.

"I'm gonna be the strongest swordfighter in the world! So I'd better go find people who are stronger than me!"

"I think you just did."

"Quiet, you!"

So they went down the road, leading the donkey, arguing and laughing.

Someday—the strongest. Someday—that dragon. The road would go ever on and on.

They were on that road, moving forward, one step at a time.

§

"Great work! You've earned a good rest."

This was the pronouncement of Guild Girl, delivered with a smile as the wagon trundled along. It must have taken some nerves to conclude everything that happened, all their trials, with these few words.

A lot really did happen, huh?

Across from her sat an adventurer in grimy armor. He nodded deliberately. "It was, indeed, rather difficult."

"Well, you were one person short of your normal party."

"Perhaps that was it."

Guild Girl giggled at this diffident response, demurely covering her mouth with her hand. Staring fixedly at the ground beside her was the priestess, her ears as alert as any elf's.

I think she's gained a little confidence.

But she still wasn't used to being openly praised. Maybe it was just as well—if she was overconfident, that would be a problem in its own right. This was adorable.

"So how'd it go with you anyway?" asked the elf, who was poking her head out the back and flicking her ears in the breeze, of that very same priestess.

"It went well!" Priestess said, nodding eagerly.

Cow Girl smirked. "Well? You were the coolest thing at the tournament!"

"O-oh, I'm not sure about that…," Priestess squeaked, her face flushing. Then, however, with a certain amount of "um, er," she managed, "But I did try my best!"

"That's what counts," said High Elf Archer, her eyes twinkling like stars. "Details! I want details!"

"I-if you don't mind, then…"

There was a delicate clearing of the throat—and then began the story of the adventure of the cleric who had impersonated the princess.

The unfamiliar outfit. The people she didn't know. The only ones she could count on were the two friends who had come with her.

Meeting the nobility, speaking to a knight, participating in the ceremony—and then the monsters had appeared.

It was a splendid tale of heroism, as fine an adventure as any there was. The only person who didn't seem to realize it was the heroine of the story.

On the driver's bench, Lizard Priest and Dwarf Shaman were

chatting about something; the others could hear the friendly rise and fall of their voices.

It was the end of a journey—calm, pleasant, quiet, and lovely.

Guild Girl took a deep breath, letting the warmth of that moment fill her chest, and then she shifted so her knees were facing the person across from her. "All right. I'd like to hear about *your* adventure, Goblin Slayer."

"Hrm," grunted a low voice from deep within the metal helmet. "Mine?"

"Yes," said Guild Girl with a smile. "Your adventure."

She stole a glance at Cow Girl. She seemed to be helping Priestess, who was gesticulating in the direction of High Elf Archer, telling the story of her exploits. *She did this! She did that!* A good flourish of the hands at the right moment could always make a story really sing.

They were not, of course, paying Guild Girl and Goblin Slayer any mind.

Well, when we get back to the west...

Then it would be her turn. Nothing wrong with cutting in line a little.

Surely no one would blame her for seizing her right to be the first to hear this person's story of adventure.

She would do it until the day he had a truly glorious tale to tell. Until she could be the first to hear about him slaying a dragon.

After all, that's how I do things!

"So what kind of adventure was it?" she asked.

"Hmm...," Goblin Slayer murmured, and after a moment's thought, he said, "There were goblins."

AFTERWORD

Hullo, Kumo Kagyu here! Did you enjoy Volume 16 of *Goblin Slayer*? I put my all into writing it, so I hope you had fun!

This time, goblins appeared in the royal capital, and Goblin Slayer accepted a quest to slay them.

And there was jousting! A tournament! *We will rock you!!*

I've been desperate to do a story with stuff like this in it—so I did! Man, jousting tournaments are great, huh? Then you have all the politicking in the background—and the mysterious knight who hides his true identity. Edward the Black Prince has nothing on him! Nor Richard I or Carl XI...

But anyway, the only thing Goblin Slayer can do is slay goblins, and so goblins he slays. He has another adventure waiting for him, one that doesn't take place on the sparkling stage of the capital proper.

There are all kinds of people in the world doing all kinds of things—that's what makes the world go round. I think many people find it difficult to accept the fact that they're just one small human being. That's what makes our fight with "the Shadow" so difficult and why overcoming that battle is so admirable.

This book is no exception to that rule. A lot of different people helped make it a reality. Everyone in the editorial division and every-one involved in publication and marketing.

Noboru Kannatuki, who provided another set of wonderful illustrations. Kousuke Kurose, who handles the manga version.

All the readers who have encouraged me, everyone who's been a fan since the web novel days, the administrators of the aggregator sites.

Not to mention my gaming buddies, the friends who are always happy to play with me.

This book owes its existence to more people than I can mention here. Thank you all, and always, so much.

Thanks to all this help, I feel like I can do more than ever. Well, my plate is always full—frankly, it's a bit much! It's weird. *Dai Katana* wrapped up just recently, so I should be feeling a little more relaxed, right…?

So recently, we've had a dungeoneering contest, the northern seas, and the capital. For the next volume, I think maybe a story in which goblins appear and have to be slain is in order.

I'll put my all into writing it, so I hope you'll enjoy it!

See you next time!